ACADEMY OF PROTECTORS

The Protector Guild Book 1

GRAY HOLBORN

ISBN: 978-1-963893-00-7

Edits: CopybyKath

Cover: DamoroDesigns

MAX

R o's fist flew straight towards my face. I ducked behind an old tree. My fingers dug into the coarse bark as the sound of his fist pounding into wood brought a smirk to my face.

He swore like a drunk sailor and unrestrained laughter spilled from my lips.

From the snap that echoed around us, I knew that at least one bone was broken. I didn't feel too bad about it though—he'd have a fully functional hand by nightfall. Ro was an extraordinarily fast healer. It made sparring with him dangerous since he was always willing to go to risky extremes.

I, on the other hand, couldn't shake off the injuries quite as quickly. It was frustrating, but at least it kept our bouts interesting and unpredictable.

"Jesus, Max. That fucking hurt." His voice was a low growl, the sound at odds with his boyish features. Beads of sweat trailed down his forehead as his brows narrowed together.

I'd pissed him off. Excellent.

I grinned at him and winked. This would be easier now. Ro sucked at fighting once he was flustered.

"Yeah, well imagine if it'd been my face. Then I'd be the one whining. Guess you'll have to move faster next time," I taunted, swinging around the tree like I was straight out of Singing in the Rain. "Besides, serves you right for stealing the last piece of pizza. I was saving that." I danced around him, my fists raised, ready for the next round.

He tilted his head from side to side until his neck let out a satisfying crack.

Rocking on the balls of my feet, I smirked up at him. Ro was huge, both in terms of height and bulk. Which meant that my five-foot-four frame definitely gave him the advantage when we trained. I was significantly faster than him though. Not that he'd ever admit it. Brothers were stubborn that way.

"You good to go another round or do you want to head back to the cabin for ice and a diaper?" I swept a few stray strands of hair from my face, relishing the cool breeze against my neck.

He bared his teeth in a grotesque caricature of a smile and pounced. He kept his right hand tucked close to his chest, but he was still a force to be reckoned with, even with only one functional arm.

I dipped low when his left fist moved towards my shoulder, but it was nothing more than a distraction. His leg swung out, sweeping my feet from under me. I landed unceremoniously on my butt, a loud thud that ricocheted through my body. There was nothing more annoying than getting your ass handed to you after a healthy dose of gloating. My pride would need some massaging later.

Before he could make his next move, I swept my leg, smiling when his mirrored thud landed next to me.

We'd been sparring for hours and both of us welcomed the short reprieve as golden leaves fell softly around us, like we were in our own personal autumnal snow globe. My head and ears were filled with the heavy thump of my heartbeat. I loved this feeling—the gentle soothing sensation of absolute exhaustion. Muscle fatigue coasted through my body like an unexpected balm.

"You going out with Jason tonight?" I asked. My eyes covertly slid to the side, satisfied with the uncharacteristic blush that colored his usually pale cheeks.

He cleared his throat nervously, subtly shifting his body away from me. "Er, who?"

My laugh bubbled over, shaking with the leftover adrenaline from the fight. "I saw you two gazing at each other adoringly last weekend at the diner, Casanova. Judging by the fact that you laid out your best plaid shirt this morning, I'd say you're trying to impress someone. Twenty bucks says it isn't me or Cyrus."

It was Saturday, the one day each week that Cyrus let us go down into town for provisions and to socialize, though he only sanctioned the former. The rest of the week was left for training and studying. And in our free time, we consumed all of the old movies and shows I'd stockpiled over the years. Just saying, my collection of eighties and nineties romantic comedies was pretty damn impressive.

But even when we went into town, there wasn't a whole lot of socializing to be done around here. Ro, Cyrus, and I lived high in the mountains. We were literally in a cabin in the woods, only no horrific or interesting stuff happened like the movies would lead you to believe. We were in complete isolation. It took a good half hour to drive to the closest town.

And even if we were near a big city, Cy didn't like us spending too much time around humans. Although, he didn't exactly allow us to spend any time around our own kind either. The man was stubborn and protective as hell. It was infuriating.

A soft thud and Ro's grunt drew my attention to my left. Cyrus stood over us as Ro wrapped his hand around the bag of ice draped across his chest.

"You knuckleheads going into town or what? I left a list on the counter." Cyrus glanced around the woods, his long black hair, peppered with gray, blowing softly in the wind. He was always hyper vigilant and checking the perimeter, even though we'd never been visited by uninvited guests in the eighteen years that I'd lived here. Incidentally, we'd never had any invited guests either. Cyrus worked his mojo to make sure no humans ever accidentally stumbled upon our super humble abode.

We were protectors—an ancient race suspected to have evolved from angels. It was speculation though, since no one had seen a true angel in centuries. Maybe even ever. Long enough that they were considered a myth at best, extinct at worst.

For the most part, we were human, just with added strength, speed, and healing powers. We also had a tendency to live longer, if left alone. But when we followed our true nature, the hunt, we died long before our human counterparts. Kind of like superheroes, only way less interesting. And without the badass costumes.

Outside of Ro and Cyrus, I'd never met another protector. Cyrus adopted me eighteen years ago, when I showed up at his doorstep in a cradle. He found Ro ten years later, in an orphanage. From what Ro could remember, his family was dead. He was left behind in a foster system that was completely unaware that the eleven-year-old it had taken in was something not quite human. The town's locals were shocked to learn that Cyrus had adopted two children. Kids were a handful at the best of times. Ro and I? We made regular kids look like saints.

And Cyrus wasn't exactly parental material. He was, to the average eye, a middle-aged recluse who did everything he could to avoid talking to people. Half of his responses were nothing more than grunts. Hence the small cabin in the middle of a mountain.

Still, here we were, at eighteen and nineteen, living with a man whose idea of affection was teaching us a new fighting style. He was our grumpy version of Mr. Miyagi. Lucky for us, his particular flavor of grump had grown on me over the years.

"Aw, you're not coming with, old man?" Ro teased. Ever since Ro turned sixteen and learned to drive, Cyrus had allowed us to go into town alone. Apparently something about earning a license satisfied him that we could handle the trip and any threats along the way. Not that there were ever any real threats, outside of overly curious townspeople. That left Cyrus free to spend his time in the cabin, in the woods, and occasionally disappear for a day or two. The man enjoyed his privacy, even from us.

Cyrus shoved Ro in the hip with his battered boot, and turned back towards the house grumbling something about teenagers.

Ro smiled at me before pulling me up with his good hand. Cyrus liked to pretend we were a burden, but we both knew he loved us. Since we were technically of age, he could have kicked us to the curb if he didn't want us around. And well, just saying, we were still here.

Half an hour later, I was freshly showered and dressed, singing along to some pop song at the top of my lungs, while Ro drove down the winding dirt road towards town. The air was crisp and my limbs were sore from a long training session. It was going to be a good day.

I ran my hand playfully through Ro's dark blond hair, smiling at the way his blue flannel top brought out the light blue color of his eyes. "You look good, Ro. James will be impressed."

"Jason," he mumbled, his face coloring slightly when he realized I'd tricked him into acknowledging his crush, "not that I'm trying to impress anyone though."

"Right, right, of course you aren't, lover boy." I added a dramatic wink, enjoying the opportunity to be playful after a long morning.

"You need to stop watching old movies, nobody actually says 'lover boy' these days, *sis*."

He was mocking but I grinned anyway. He didn't refer to me as his sister often, but it always made me feel warm and gooey when he did. Unlike me, he knew his family before they died and he joined our ragtag group in the woods. He remembered what his mother looked like, the kinds of things she loved to do, her favorite perfume. But me? He was the closest thing I had to family, other than Cyrus.

We even kind of looked like brother and sister.

If you squinted really, really hard. Or, you know, didn't look at us at all.

Everything about Rowan was fair: his eyes were pale like the afternoon sky and his skin only had color when the sun darkened it. Despite my ability to spark his frustration, he was generally calm, rational, level-headed. It always made me laugh because while my black hair and brown complexion resembled Cy's more than his, they were two peas in a pod. I looked like the bio-daughter, but Ro acted like the bio-son. It was a weird thread that connected the three of us together, like an unusually-constructed puzzle.

Ro also had an 'awareness' about him. That's what Cy always said anyway, and usually only as a way to highlight my lack thereof. I just wasn't as serious and paranoid about the world.

"Yeah, well, whatever. You just let me know if you want me to disappear and give you and Jason some alone time." I opened my window slightly, soaking in the fresh, crisp smell of fall. Pretty soon, we'd be dealing with snow and ice, so it was important to appreciate the season while we had it. Training in the dead of winter was absolute agony.

"Yes, because clearly you'd be doing me the favor by hanging around town alone." He eyed my black dress and leggings as I pulled the hem down, uncomfortable in the unusually dressy outfit. Cyrus thought fancy clothes were pointless. And I mean, since we didn't really go anywhere, they kind of were. I was typically lounging around in leggings or sweatpants, always paired with a raggedy tank or t-shirt for sparring. My favorites were the ones Ro tossed out—they had holes and faded print, but were soft with wear and fell to my knees.

While it was amusing to poke fun at Ro, since he got embarrassed so easily, he wasn't the only one to notice the new family in town. Jason had a younger brother, Michael, who was the best-looking boy I'd seen in real life. At least I thought so, anyway. He looked just like the nice-boy jocks in all those CW shows. And, well, when you spent most of your time living virtually alone on a mountain, you took notice when fresh meat moved to town.

Our first stop was always the post office, to check if Cyrus had any mail. He almost never did, unless bills and advertisements counted, but today there was a crinkled letter with no return address. Ro and I tried holding it up to the light, to see if we could read it without opening. The technique seemed to work frequently enough in spy flicks, but we had no such luck. I shoved the letter to the bottom of my bag, hoping that Cyrus would share it with us when he opened it.

We played guessing games all the way to the diner, creating elaborate stories about who could be writing to him. I was secretly counting on it being a long-lost love interest, with some tragic backstory. In all the time I'd lived with him, Cyrus had never gone on a date. I'd caught him checking out a few of the women in town a couple of times, but nothing ever came of it.

And it wasn't like he was terrible looking for an old dude. He somehow managed to make long hair look badass instead of homely, and he was strong and lean from all the sparring and training. He had a slight limp from an old injury, but it kind of added to his mysterious persona.

Ro opened the door for me, and I sank into that burning feeling against my skin as my body transitioned from the crisp air outside, into the overly heated diner atmosphere. The diner itself wasn't anything to write home about, but we loved it all the same. Truthfully, it was probably my favorite place in the world, and felt just as much like home as our cabin did.

The countertops were clean, but slick with years of grease buildup and stained an odd yellow color—the kind of yellow you just knew beyond a shadow of a doubt wasn't the original color. The padding on each of the booths had a few holes and burn spots from the days customers could smoke inside. I usually found myself distractedly picking at the pieces of tape meant to keep the stuffing from falling out. Darlene, our favorite server, was working as usual and she had two steaming cups of coffee ready for us as soon as we made it to our favorite table. Ro and I both ordered our usual—steak with a side of fries—and discreetly searched the diner for the two newish faces we hoped to find.

Jason spotted Ro almost immediately, and made a beeline for our table as soon as their eyes connected.

"Hi. Rowan, right?" he asked, fiddling with the hem of his dark wool sweater. He was nervous, and I just about melted into a puddle from the cuteness. Jason looked a lot like his brother, with tousled blond hair and bright green eyes. His angles were a bit more defined, and something about the way he held himself just made him seem older than he was, like he'd experienced so much in his short life. "I'm Jason. I think we met last weekend." He glanced around, rubbing the back of his neck, like he was checking to see if we were being watched. "I haven't really seen you around since then."

"Oh, that's because we live outside of town and only come in on the wee—" I cut myself off when I caught sight of Ro's glare. Right, Jason wasn't talking to me. In fact, he hadn't even so much as glanced in my direction.

"You can call me Ro. This is Max." He nodded towards me. "Would you like to eat with us?" Ro scooted over to make room on his side of the booth, his expression open, hopeful.

I wiggled my eyebrows at Ro before his quick glare told me to cool it.

"Yeah sure." He sat down, letting out a long relieved breath. His eyes brightened considerably, taking his cues from Ro. "Would it be okay if my brother joined us in a bit? He's finishing some things up at work, but he's supposed to meet me here soon for some food. He'll be stoked to meet some new people in town."

"Totally!" Ro and I echoed each other, giant smiles on our faces. Clearly neither of us was very good at playing it cool. But tonight was shaping up to be better than we'd hoped, the puzzle pieces falling together perfectly, just like a romance novel.

I absentmindedly scratched at the scar on my wrist, forcing myself to sit back and let Jason and Ro get to know each other without my butting in. My fingers curved over the smooth, familiar lines that almost resembled a star. Protectors didn't really scar, but I'd had this one since the day I showed up at Cy's.

I choked on my water when Michael walked over, embarrassing myself as a few droplets dribbled down my chin before I could catch them. While Jason was a lot more hesitant in his approach, Michael exuded confidence and excitement. He sat down next to me after officially introducing himself, and I twisted my brain into knots trying to come up with things to say. Jason and Ro seemed to have no problem finding conversational topics, but Michael and I mostly sat in an awkward silence while I scarfed down my steak. Which was unusual for me. Generally, I never shut up. According to Cy, it was my most annoying quality. I took a deep breath and decided to be myself, trying to mimic Ro's relaxed pose.

"So um, how do you like it here?" I cleared my throat and stared at the smooth skin between Michael's eyes, too nervous to look him in the eyes but wanting to fake confidence by looking in their general direction. "Where are you guys from? Are you going to college?" I glanced at Ro, noticing the way his eyes were slightly bugging at me. Right. I was rambling. Bad habit of mine. "Sorry, that was too many questions in a row, wasn't it?" I cleared my throat. "I should've paused a bit in between," I added, mostly to myself.

Michael smiled, and my stomach did this swirly thing when he looked over at me and chuckled. "I'm liking it better now, we're from southern California, and no."

"California? That's so cool. Do you surf?" Hollywood made it seem like everyone from California surfed. His tousled blond hair definitely fit the stereotype.

"No we lived on the east side of the state, plus I'm kind of afraid of the ocean." He ruffled his hair and looked at me from the side of his eye. "Not being able to see what you're walking on top of sort of wigs me out, you know?"

I nodded enthusiastically, even though I didn't really know what he meant.

With the ice broken, we sat in pleasant conversation for the rest of the meal and I did my best not to put my foot in my mouth. Dating was one thing Cyrus and Ro didn't really bother teaching me. All I had to go on was movies and books. Not for the first time, I found myself suddenly wishing for girlfriends to hangout and chat with.

"Could I maybe get your phone number, Max?" Michael cleared his throat, and I smiled at the nervous tremble in his words. Maybe he sucked at this whole dating thing too? And maybe we could help each other and learn together?

"No, sorry." I paused, realizing how that sounded. "I mean, not no because I don't want you to have it, but no because you can't."

My cheeks reddened and I kicked Ro in the shin when I heard his laughter crack through the awkward silence.

"I mean, I don't have a phone. So I can't give you my number. Because, you know, since I don't have a phone, I don't have a number...to give...to you," I finished awkwardly, mentally smacking myself with a hammer and hoping like hell that I wasn't as bright red as I felt.

Jason and Ro were both laughing behind their hands, and I shrank a few inches into the booth, silently promising myself that I'd kick Ro's ass tomorrow during training.

"We're in town every Saturday." Ro said. "I think what Max is trying so eloquently to say, is that maybe we could all just grab dinner again next weekend and go from there?"

Why was Ro so much better than me at this? It wasn't like he had much more practice when it came to socializing or flirting. I pushed my jealousy at his easy conversation down, determined to take notes for next time.

Michael nodded, a bemused expression on his face. "Yeah, next Saturday works." His hand brushed against mine and my nerves disappeared a bit, which was odd. In novels the heroine's stomach was supposed to explode with butterflies at the first touch of her hero. "Could I walk you to your car?"

I averted my eyes and tried to stop the grin from exploding all over my face. "Yeah sure." I turned back to Ro. "Meet you there in a few?"

We threw some money on the table and made our way out the door. I didn't have too much time to kill since we still had to grab some groceries before the store closed, but Michael and I took the long way, walking around the town square a bit before we made our way back to the mouth of the alley where our car was parked. Sometime between leaving the restaurant and crossing the street, he grabbed my right hand. My first instinct was to kick him in the knees, but I realized at the last second that this was normal teenager stuff and I didn't have to worry about fighting tactics.

Then again, maybe he'd be impressed by my reflexes?

"How come you guys only come down from the cabin on the weekends? Is your dad really strict or something?"

I wasn't totally sure how to handle that question. I was, however, perfectly sure that telling him we spent our time training to kill supernatural creatures wasn't normal conversation for a human.

"Yes, he's just really overprotective," I lied. Really, he just didn't want us getting too close to humans. And considering that's all Ro and I seemed interested in doing when we came into town, he had good reason to be worried. Cyrus enjoyed solitude, but Ro and I craved a social life. I looked around for a safer subject. I knew that dating a human would come with some lying, but I wanted to avoid it as much as I could. "Your brother mentioned you were at work earlier. What do you do?"

"Currently I'm working at the auto repair shop down the road, but I'm taking some online classes. Hopefully in a year or two, I can get my associate's degree and apply to a four-year school. That's my endgame, anyway." He shrugged before leaning his back against our truck. What about you?"

Ro and I were homeschooled. Cyrus taught us traditional subjects, but he also made sure we understood the basics when it came to the hell realm. Still, we both knew that as protectors, we couldn't have real careers. And, honestly, now that we were both technically adults, we needed to start thinking about our own endgames. If I had a choice in the matter, I'd spend all my extra time reading, but I didn't think that could ever really count as a career. Unfortunately, the same was probably true for being a professional Netflix-watcher. If I were human, I'd probably want to be some sort of scholar. I loved fighting, but if I wasn't doing that, I was just as happy with my nose in a book or computer.

Michael cleared his throat loudly, which I think was a sign that I'd been silent for too long. Sorting through my head for human careers, I landed on one I wouldn't hate. "I guess I'd like to be a veterinarian one day. I really love animals."

He smiled, his features brightening with interest. It was the best I could come up with, since I couldn't exactly tell him that my career would involve saving unsuspecting humans from supernatural creatures that escaped from hell. Then again, maybe he watched Buffy—in which case, he might think I was kind of cool?

Our conversation grew easier, as he cycled through questions and lighter topics, and I carefully wove through and around them the best that I could. After a long, rambling monologue about one of my favorite books, I looked up at Michael only to find that he'd moved a few inches closer, his nose just a breath away from mine. Before I had a chance to say anything, his lips pressed against the corner of my mouth.

It was an awkward first kiss, but he corrected his positioning after a moment, enveloping my lips more fully. His tongue parted the seam of my mouth, and I tasted the baked cod he'd ordered for dinner.

Not exactly great first-kiss flavor.

Still, in a town this small, I had to take what I could get. I waited for my stomach to explode with butterflies or for a light to ding in my head signaling that he was the one. Would my lips be swollen? Romance novels always went on and on about swollen lips after a kiss. While all of this ran through my head as our lips collided awkwardly, all I could focus on was how I would never order the cod from the diner if I could help it.

He gasped into my mouth, a nanosecond before he was torn from my lips. Before I could make a corny comment about how I literally took his breath away, his body flew back into the truck and I watched, mesmerized, as a giant brown wolf dragged him further into the alleyway behind the diner. The wolf had to be about two hundred pounds, and came up to my chest while standing on all four legs...which meant it would be a lot taller than me if it were standing on its hind legs. The bright yellow glow in its eyes told me everything I needed to know.

This was a straight up werewolf.

2

MAX

Wolfie was not going to steal the date I'd waited so long for. Not on my watch.

I grabbed the knife I kept in the lining of my boot and pounced. My feet pounded against the gravelly road as I bound after them, ready to rescue my soon-to-be boyfriend in a grand heroic gesture.

I was all about flipping the narrative.

Harsh steps behind me beat in a familiar rhythm. Ro reached the wolf almost at the same moment I did. He must've been secretly eavesdropping on us. Hopefully none of the other townspeople noticed the wolf. There was a reason humans stored books about them in the fantasy section—werewolves weren't usually this brazen and obvious with their attacks.

My blade sank into the wolf's flank and I twisted before pulling it out and repeating the maneuver. Ro grabbed Michael and threw him, his heightened strength unintentionally knocking him out in the process. Which was probably for the best. Too many witnesses wasn't good news for us. While Ro fought to get a good grip on the wolf, I pulled my silver-plated blade back and struck into the creature's heart. Hard.

And missed, hitting its shoulder instead. Target practice was so much easier when the target didn't fidget about so much.

The wolf bucked Ro across the alley and came charging towards me, an annoyed glint in its eye. Could werewolves be annoyed? I wasn't really sure, but this one sure looked it. The wolf growled low but, oddly, didn't strike. Instead, it cocked its head and looked at me with what I can only describe as curiosity. It seemed so...human. I positioned the knife and bounced softly on the balls of my feet, ready to spring and go full on Van Helsing on its ass.

Before I had the chance though, a huge black dog, as big as a small pony, beat me to it. It tore into the wolf's neck, and with a whimper and growl, the werewolf sprang off into the forest, sparing one strange glance back at me before its yellow eyes disappeared from sight.

The black dog was slightly larger than the wolf. It walked over to me, bowed its head, licked a small cut on my arm and ran off in the opposite direction.

Animals were so weird. Maybe I really would be a vet.

"Just so you know, I'm totally taking credit for that win," I yelled after it, wiping off the drool. The cut would be healed within the hour. I didn't have Ro's speedy superhuman healing, but I was no slouch.

I stood, flabbergasted, until Ro caught up, limping slightly on his left foot. We checked quickly to make sure Michael was still breathing, only to find Jason at the mouth of the alley staring at us like we were a couple of serial killers. I tucked my knife not-so-discreetly into my boot, as if hiding the evidence would suddenly make this whole thing disappear.

"Wh-what the hell was that?" He pushed past us and ran to his brother. With his finger on Michael's pulse point, he shot us a terrified look and grabbed his phone. Judging by the fact that his fingers only pressed on three numbers, he was calling the police.

Okay, apparently Jason wasn't a fan of Buffy. Good to know. Ro could definitely do better.

Ro mumbled something about rabid wolves in the woods this time of the year and rabies, before shuffling me back towards the car. Michael would be okay. Probably. Humans were so freaking fragile.

On the bright side, werewolves couldn't turn humans. Contrary to popular literary beliefs, their bite couldn't transform a human into a wolf. There was no way, as far as I knew, to turn a human into anything even remotely supernatural, so I had no idea why they were always so terrified of that in the movies. A werewolf could theoretically turn a protector into a wolf, but it was rare. Generally though, most protectors who were bitten either died from the bite or they didn't exhibit any effects at all. Werewolfism was hard to predict.

Magic wasn't really a science in that sense.

The wound on Michael's leg from where the beast grabbed him appeared pretty shallow. Honestly, Jason probably needed to worry more about the head injury, but I didn't want to call Ro out on that.

Our bodies were still pumping adrenaline from our first real supernatural encounter. Not wanting to waste time or field questions, we skipped the grocery store and sped home.

"Sorry, Ro. I didn't mean to ruin your date. Jason looked pretty pissed." I traced indiscernible shapes in the dust of the car window. The night had started out so promising. So *normal*.

"Don't be sorry, it wasn't your fault." Ro exhaled loud and hard. "And to be honest, I don't know that it was so bad. The werewolf part was obviously not great. But I'm not sure how much I liked Jason because I liked him, and how much I liked him because he's only the second gay guy I've met in this town. And the *only* gay guy under fifty."

I frowned in sympathy, not sure what to say.

"Besides, it's foolish to think it would work, being with a human." Ro shrugged his shoulders, glancing briefly at me as the car wound up the familiar path. "We can't hide who we are forever, Max."

That was true, Cyrus was always warning us about humans. And he would not be happy to hear about our trip—the part about the werewolf or the part about us getting cozy with two humans in a pseudo double-date. Protector-human relationships weren't *exactly* encouraged. But that's okay. At least I had my first kiss. Even if the best part of it was the resulting fight. I'd never seen a werewolf before.

For the first time, I felt like an actual protector.

"A WEREWOLF? YOU'RE CERTAIN?" CYRUS WAS PACING AROUND the living room, wearing down our already-worn-down rug even more. The cabin itself was small, but there was a warmness about it that I loved.

"Yes, its eyes were glowing and it looked way too big and intelligent for a regular wolf." Mentally, I traced through all the information I'd learned about werewolves from Cyrus's books. There wasn't much known about them. The internet was rife with made-up information, and Cyrus only had a few books in the house from his time working in official protector capacity for The Guild. Still, I did know that they came from the hell realm and fed primarily on animals they caught in the woods. Werewolves were generally able to control their transformations, but they were far more volatile and unpredictable in their wolf forms. Still, it was incredibly rare for them to show up in the middle of a town filled with humans. Secrecy kept them alive. If humans had concrete evidence that they were real, werewolves would be in serious trouble.

Ro nodded, confirming my diagnosis. He had mastered the art of talking without words. I wasn't there yet.

"And it didn't kill the human? Or seriously injure you two?" Cyrus dragged his hand through his dark locks, his fingers catching on a few tangles. He could use a good brush, the Tarzan look wasn't really working for him at the moment. Cyrus wasn't usually filled with this much nervous energy and I had a feeling it would be a long while before we were allowed back into town without him. And since he avoided going into town like the plague, Ro and I would be spending the next few months as recluses.

Cyrus's eyes locked onto us, like he was scanning for injuries.

So much for my big date next weekend. I'd spent the whole trip home mentally running through ways I could subtly convince Michael to order something other than fish. I wanted a do-over.

Then again, the odds of Michael wanting to see me after being attacked by a wolf in my presence weren't exactly great. And Jason didn't *exactly* seem impressed with our participation in the encounter either. I was starting to understand why protector-human relationships were so taboo. Dating was already complicated enough. Hiding your whole world from your partner? That was just unnecessary trouble to throw into the mix.

"Oh," I chirped, rubbing a hand over my face. The adrenaline was starting to wear off and I desperately wanted to curl up with a good book and hot cup of tea. "Also there was a big dog. It sort of saved me. I think."

Cyrus stopped his excessive pacing and turned to look at me like I was dense. It was an expression he used frequently when talking to me. I had learned not to be offended.

"A big dog? Saved you from a werewolf?"

The familiar line between his brows made an appearance and I blushed under the doubt in his coal eyes. "I mean it was, like, a really, *really* big dog. So, you know, way more believable, right?"

Ro shook his head, a grin stealing over his face as he glanced between me and Cyrus. "She's telling the truth, Cy. The dog was huge. As soon as it bit the wolf and sent it running, it pranced over to her, bowed, licked her, and left us. It was like a weird, overgrown house pet. I've never seen anything like it."

I beamed. I was practically Dr. Dolittle.

"How huge?" Cyrus seemed way more interested in the dog than he'd been in the wolf, which had my stomach fluttering nervously.

"Like, small-pony-sized. Or like, you know, giant-dog-sized. Way bigger than Mrs. Dell's pug that walks around town sometimes." Words were not my strong suit when I was feeling anxious. Between talking to a boy I liked, an awkwardly fishy kiss, a werewolf attack, and Cyrus's unusually heightened energy, I was doomed. Not my fault.

Cyrus looked to Ro in exasperation, clearly aware that he wouldn't get a useful answer from me. I rolled my eyes. At least we had a system worked out.

"I know what you're thinking, it wasn't another werewolf. It was at least four or five feet tall while on all of its legs, probably close to two hundred pounds. Definitely not a human breed of dog, but kind of looked like an enlarged Newfoundland, if that helps," Ro reported, the spitting image of a soldier reporting for duty.

Cyrus's lips thinned into a tight line. He nodded his head, his expression growing distant. "I see." He looked at me and, thinking better of it, turned back to Ro. "Anything else?"

Annoyed with being brushed off, I dug my hand into my black bag, pulling out the crumpled letter from the post office. "Yeah, you got mail."

෨෨

RO AND I EXCHANGED GLANCES WHILE CYRUS READ THE letter. And then read it again. And again. With each pass, his eyes darkened and his posture grew more stiff. It didn't appear that long, so I had no idea why he needed so many passes over it. I could have read a whole chapter and taken notes by now.

Finally, he looked up at us, his mouth set in a grim line. "Pack your things."

I glanced at Ro again before turning back to Cyrus. "Er, why?"

"We're leaving, and I'm guessing you'll want your things." Cyrus sprang to action, gathering his rather sparse collection of items around the living room and kitchen, before he moved to his weapons room, which was significantly less sparse.

"Care to tell us where we're going, Cy?" Ro rolled the words slowly over his tongue, as if he were talking to a toddler.

"The Protector Guild. I've been offered a position. By default, you two will be accepted as students. If there really are werewolves in this area, there's no use pretending that hiding out is doing you any good. So, we'll try this instead for a bit. I've taught you what I can, now you need formal training."

"W-what?" I asked. The Protector Guild housed the most elite training academy for protectors. According to Cyrus's books, they only accepted the best of the best. Seeing as how Ro and I were completely segregated from the North American community of protectors, I highly doubted we came anywhere near the traditional standards for their students.

"We leave tomorrow night. Anything you haven't packed by then, gets left behind." Cyrus's voice echoed over the clatter of metal as he tore all his weapons from the walls and threw them haphazardly onto a large sheet. I cringed. He really should be wrapping them each individually and taking proper care of them. Ro and I watched, stunned, as he gathered the ends of the sheet together, creating a makeshift sack that he dragged towards the door. "I mean it."

I looked at Ro, watching his blue eyes widen, and then we jumped into action, gathering our meager collection of clothes, books, and weapons before Cyrus had the chance to leave them, or us, behind.

3

MAX

After driving for two hours, we pulled up to a large gate that opened as soon as our car came within a few feet of it. A winding road led us through a forest and an odd collection of small buildings for at least a mile before we reached what I can only describe as a mansion. Or a small town housed under a single roof.

The place was huge and looked like an old castle. According to Cyrus, The Protector Guild was hidden away in northern Montana, protected by spells that ensured no human would ever find it. The spell part didn't shock me. The place looked like a freaking magic castle you'd only hear about in fairy tales. Though I guess, by now, I shouldn't be surprised to learn that fairy tales were always partially settled in truth. I did just encounter a werewolf and pony-dog after all.

When we reached the front door, a man with graying brown hair and a whiskery beard grasped Cyrus closely. I studied them both, tracing the similar square jaw, lean muscular build, and black intelligent eyes. This man was related to Cyrus.

"Brother, it's been too long," he said.

Well, that was confirmed quickly.

The man looked over at Ro and me. "And I guess that makes you two my sort of niece and nephew, eh?"

"What the hell, Cyrus, you have a family? Why didn't you ever tell us? And your family lives at Guild Headquarters? Also, why didn't you tell me that this place looks kind of like it was crafted straight out of a fairytale?"

Ro slammed his palm against my mouth, cutting off my questions a moment later than he probably should have. Cyrus always said that the one thing he failed to teach me was how to create a filter between my thoughts and words. So really, it was his fault. Nerves did weird things to my brain.

The man laughed, the deep rolling sound similar to Cyrus's, though I'd only heard him full-out laugh a few times in all of my eighteen years. "Call me Seamus."

Cyrus gave me that stop-being-asinine look that I was so familiar with. "Seamus, this is Rowan and Maxi—" Cyrus's voice cut off as I stepped on his foot. He knew I hated my full name. And that was also his fault. He was the one who named me. "I mean Max. She prefers Max. Anyway, these are the kids I raised —against my better judgment." He muttered the last part softly to himself, but we all heard it anyway.

"Excellent. You both will be staying in the student housing. I'll have people send your bags up to your rooms in a bit. In the meantime, dinner just started, so let's grab a bite to eat while I explain how The Guild operates. I'm sure you're all starving." Seamus moved his hand, a gesture signaling us to enter the creepy, beautiful castle ahead of him. It seemed oddly poetic that a place housing people trained to kill vampires, werewolves, and all sorts of fantastical beasts looked like Dracula's castle.

I nudged Ro, making it clear I wanted him to go first. We'd never been around protectors before, and I was woman enough to admit that the thought of suddenly being thrust into the community had me all sorts of nervous.

The doors opened into a huge entrance hall. Or was it a foyer? I think that was the fancy term for entrance hall. Anyway, it was huge and lit with a giant chandelier that threw chaotic but beautiful patterns of light around the room. The rugs lining the halls were a rich burgundy that matched the accents painted along the walls. It was beautiful, and so very different from the decor I was used to.

Seamus led us through the hall, whispering softly to Cyrus. I watched from behind, comparing the two brothers. Cyrus was taller, but his slight limp affected his posture, making him look to be about the same height. He refused to talk about how he got the limp in the first place, but it had to be a hell of a story. Protectors didn't incur permanent damage easily.

Seamus turned left and opened another door into a huge room. This new room was strange, in part because it seemed completely modernized, whereas the castle and entrance hall looked like they dated back to the Victorian period.

The room was at least four times larger than our entire cabin, and lined with food stations. The main floor was filled with scattered tables and chairs, and a musical hum of people engaging in various conversations. As soon as we stepped in, hundreds of eyes turned in our direction. I slid quietly behind Ro, happy to let his extra height and bulk shield me from the attention. Maybe I was more introverted than I realized.

As Seamus led us towards an empty table, I noticed that everyone was staring at Cyrus, not us. The realization calmed my nerves, but heightened my curiosity. Why would they be so interested in him? He was just a grumpy old man whose idea of fun involved making us run ten miles in the rain. In the middle of the night.

The whispers filtering through the hall, suggested that they knew exactly who he was. Clearly I didn't.

Seamus pulled my chair out, waiting to seat himself until I was comfortably settled in the metal chair.

"On second thought, Seamus, why don't you let Ro and Max grab their food now. That'll give us a second to catch up. It's been a long time." The firm look in Cyrus's eye was one I was familiar with—it usually meant 'do as I say, don't ask any questions.' Clearly Seamus was familiar with it as well. He pointed us in the direction of food without another thought.

"We can have whatever we want?" I asked, salivating at the thought. The room smelled divine. Cy wasn't exactly a Food-Network-quality chef. He'd mastered boxed spaghetti over the years, but not much more than that.

Seamus nodded, smiling indulgently.

Not waiting for more confirmation, Ro and I were off.

"My eyes aren't going right? That's Cyrus Bentley?" A pale boy with freckles whispered to his friend as we passed, his eyes wide with shock.

"If it's not him, it's someone who looks a helluva lot like him, anyway," the friend responded, not even bothering to lower his voice.

I followed Ro towards the nearest stack of trays, glued so closely to him that I was practically tripping him. "Ro, why is everyone staring at Cyrus?"

"Not everyone." Ro's expression was filled with curiosity as he discreetly glanced across the room.

I followed his line of sight and was met with a pair of brown eyes, set in the most strikingly handsome face I'd ever seen. He had to be several years older than me, his dark eyes speaking of a level of maturity and experience I hadn't reached yet. His hair was black, longer on top and shorter on the sides. A layer of black fuzz shadowed his square jaw, and a slight bump on his nose told me he'd likely broken it before and hadn't had it properly set before it healed.

Which was strange. Protectors healed so fast, it made sense to just break it again and reshape it. My eyes took in the clear, olive-toned skin covering muscular arms. When my gaze made it back up to his eyes, I saw that he was giving me a sharp look filled with distrust and a strong dislike. The second that our eyes met, sharp chills ran down my spine, pushing my anxiety into overdrive.

Maybe Cyrus wasn't popular among the protectors? And we, by association, were also going to be unpopular?

Great, first chance to make friends—ever—and we were already coming in at a disadvantage. I cleared my throat, uncomfortable under the man's scrutiny, and started distractedly piling food on my plate.

When we made it back to our table, Seamus's face split in a wide grin. "I see you like dessert, Max."

My eyebrows bunched in confusion, until I looked down and found that my dinner consisted of various pies, cakes, and cookies. So much for a nutritional meal.

"Er, um, yeah," I said, frowning. "Cyrus doesn't really keep our place stocked with sweets." I unenthusiastically grabbed one of the cookies. Truthfully, I didn't have much of a sweet tooth, and I eyed Ro's collection of salad, steak, chicken, and potatoes enviously. After a lifetime of training, I knew which foods kept my energy reserves up. Sugar didn't do it for me.

He rolled his eyes, trading a piece of my chocolate cake for half of his steak. I squeezed his hand under the table in gratitude.

We ate while Cyrus and Seamus got up to fill their own trays. I was conscious of a pair of eyes boring into my back, and I knew, if I turned around, who they'd belong to. After finishing half of Ro's steak, I grabbed a pile of potatoes and slid him some of the peanut butter pie I'd accidentally grabbed.

"Thanks, my dude." I laughed around a mouthful of potatoes, fueling my anxiety with carbs. Carbs cured everything, it was a fact. Some girls dreamed of swimming in pools of diamonds. And then there was me. I would happily dive into a mountain of pasta instead.

Seamus sat next to me, his plate full with what looked like a much more balanced meal than mine, and I caught myself eyeing his vegetables with envy. I had a serious love affair with broccoli and spinach, but would be perfectly fine with never seeing a piece of chocolate again. I blamed my weird taste buds on my fear of Cyrus's disappointment and my obsession with Popeye growing up.

"Cyrus tells me that you've both been taught various fighting techniques, and have some basic knowledge of the parameters of the hell realm?" Seamus politely cut his steak into neat little bites. He seemed so refined and polished in comparison to Cyrus. Had they grown up together? Or was Cyrus just raised by wolves?

Ro and I nodded around mouthfuls. We'd all but traded plates at this point. Sometimes brothers were the fucking best.

Cyrus cleared his throat, his eyes meeting mine before turning towards his own brother. "Their, er, knowledge of hell is pretty limited. But their fighting is up to par with your best, I'm sure."

Seamus narrowed his eyes slightly and titled his head, studying Cyrus with curiosity. "Knowing that, I think I'll keep you both with your age groups for the physical training. We may need to assign you both some tutors for the theoretical stuff though, to make sure you understand how The Guild runs. I'll know more tomorrow, once Cyrus and I have had more time to hammer out the basics. Any questions?"

"Uh yeah," I stammered, jealously eyeing the slice of pizza on a girl's plate as she walked by us. "What do you all do at this place?"

Cyrus rolled his eyes, but Seamus smiled. Guess it was clear who won all the manners in their family.

"Great question." Seamus dropped his fork before dabbing a napkin at each corner of his mouth. "This is the North American home base for protectors. That's why it's so huge here, and why the campus runs a few miles in each direction. We have the academy portion, which works on training and instructing our young adults, obviously. But most of our resources are devoted to our research unit, which tries to gain more knowledge about the supernatural creatures we hunt. And then of course, there's our operations base, which houses and manages the many teams of protectors that actually work on, well, protecting." Seamus nodded towards Cyrus. "He's here to help us manage and train a few field teams, since we've been experiencing some heightened supernatural activity lately." He smiled warmly at me. Why was he so much nicer than Cy? "Other questions?"

Ro shook his head no, but there was absolutely no way I was passing up the open offer to learn more. Cyrus was so tightlipped about all things Guild-related, and I was ready to soak up the information like a damn eager sponge.

"Yeah, why does everyone keep staring at Cy?"

Ro and Cyrus both groaned into their food—a pretty common occurrence during our meal time if I was being honest.

Seamus laughed, the warmness in it reaching all the way up to his eyes. "You were right, Cyrus, she is a very curious girl." He turned back towards me. "Let's just say Cyrus is a very, *very* well-known fighter and people are just surprised to see him here after so many years in solitude. It's been a long time since he's participated in anything relating to The Guild."

I shrugged, made sense I guess, with all the time he devoted to training us in fighting strategies and techniques. Maybe he was like the golden child chosen one of his day. The main character hero of The Guild.

Seamus nodded to someone behind us. "Eli, come here for a second. I want to introduce you to a few people."

A boy, well, I guess man was a better way to phrase it as he looked to be in his early to mid-twenties, walked up to our table and my breath hitched. He had light, shaggy brown hair that fell just above warm, honey-brown eyes. There was a mischievous edge lurking there in the amber pools—it drew me in like a magnet.

Were protectors, on average, all good looking? Maybe it was the universe's way of saying 'thank you for saving everyone from the baddies'—here, take some pretty. His eyes fell on me and I felt my cheeks heat when he lifted his lips in a cocky grin. The top lip was slightly fuller than the bottom and I had a difficult time looking away. He was trouble.

"This is my son, Eli." Seamus lifted a brow at Eli's predatory smirk and shook his head. "Eli, this is your Uncle Cyrus. And his adopted wards, Ro and Max. Treat them like your cousins." He growled the last part in a low, deep voice that I suspected was meant for only Eli, but we all heard. Protector senses made it almost impossible for whispering to be effective.

Eli gripped Cyrus's and Ro's hands firmly, but when his hand met mine, his eyes darkened, directing all of his attention to me. I squirmed under the appraisal.

"Pleasure to meet you all." His voice was deep and smooth, and I looked back to Ro, uncomfortable with the prolonged eye contact and the feel of his coarse, strong hand around mine.

"Eli's part of one of our elite teams here. They'll be helping with training some of the recruits for the next couple of months, in between their assignments." Seamus turned back to Eli. "Can you show Ro and Max to their rooms?"

When Eli nodded, Seamus slid him an envelope which I assumed had the details of our living assignments. My stomach lurched. I'd shared a tiny cabin with Cyrus and Ro my entire life. Hell, mine and Ro's rooms were separated by nothing but an old, worn sheet. I wasn't comfortable with the idea of living away from them, even if we were still technically housed under the same roof. We might as well be living in different zip codes, for as big as this place was.

I wouldn't admit that out loud though. I wanted to play the badass protector card for as long as I could.

Eli turned and led us out of the dining hall. My eyes lingered for a brief moment on the man with dark, assessing eyes before I forced myself to follow.

We wound through several hallways and up two different staircases. Each room we passed was more elaborate and breathtaking than the last. I'd need a map if I had any hope of finding my way around tomorrow.

"My father says that you and Cyrus grew up in isolation, away from most protectors. Is that true?" Eli asked. His pace was lazy and self-assured, and I had a feeling he could find any room in the building with his eyes shut.

How different would my life be if I'd grown up here like him? If Ro and I spent our childhood learning about the hell realm and studying the fantastical creatures we were meant to kill? Why had Cyrus hidden himself away for so long?

"Uh, yeah." I cleared my throat and tried to track every turn we took. I'd want breakfast in the morning, and getting lost was not on my to-do list. "Just us. Cy got the letter to move here only yesterday." I looked from wall to wall as we walked, trying to soak up as much of the beautiful art and decor as I could. I was used to such a simple life in the cabin. The fanciest thing I'd ever seen in real life was the new Quickie Mart with one of those automatic paper towel dispensers. Everything about this place screamed lavish excess, like I was living in a movie. Apparently demon hunting paid well.

"Well, if you both trained for most of your lives with him, I imagine you'll have no trouble catching up in your sparring classes. He's a bit of a god amongst our people. Especially those of us who focus on field work."

"Is your father in charge of training the students?" Ro asked, his strides matching Eli's one for one.

Eli smiled, and my stomach fluttered at the brief glimpse of straight, white teeth. His smile lit up his whole face, turning him from a predator into just a boy. A very, *very* good looking boy. "My father doesn't usually lead the student training. Generally, he focuses on managing and training some of the elite teams. The headmistress, who usually works with her bondmates to train students, is out of the country meeting with the heads of the other Guild locations. I imagine it's why my father called Cyrus in. We're a bit strapped here right now and could use more qualified hands on deck."

"Bondmates?" I stuttered over the word. "As in plural? And

mates as in, like, animals?" I tried not to show the disgust I was feeling at the idea. It just seemed so animalistic and, I don't know, imprisoning?

"You'll learn quickly that female protectors are relatively rare, and that protectors in general are quickly declining in numbers. For those who are particularly powerful, like the headmistress, it isn't uncommon to have one or even two bondmates. It's built-in protection and evolutionary planning—not necessarily romantic. For our people, bondmates are the symbol of complete trust and camaraderie. If you're chosen to bond, there is a complex ceremony to initiate the process."

I wrinkled my nose, but didn't respond. Cyrus never spoke of mates—or anything relating to the social lives of protectors—and the idea sounded primitive and forced. Were female protectors just treated like baby incubators? Because hell no, that would not fly with me.

Ro took one look at me and laughed. "Don't worry, Max. All the luck in the world to any man who thinks he can take care of you while still retaining his manhood." He laughed softly, but I caught the way he studied Eli with curiosity and a hint of trepidation. Blood relatives or not, Ro was still just a protective older brother when it came to guys. I'm pretty sure the only reason he even let me go on a walk with Michael was because he was trying to get close to Jason and didn't want to seem like too much of a prude. And look how that turned out.

"Anyway," Eli added, "My team will be helping with some of the training while she's gone, along with my father and Cyrus if they're needed. Trust me, you'll be glad. The Headmistress can be a bit of a handful." He shook his head and chuckled before turning yet another corner.

"On a scale of Miss Honey to Miss Trunchbull, where would you say she falls?" I asked, struggling to keep up with their long strides.

At Eli's curious stare, Ro laughed before explaining. "You'll get used to it. Her only companions until I came around were books, TV shows, and movies. Most of which are outdated. And it's not like the addition of me exactly extended her social circle into what counts as normal."

Eli nodded, but didn't respond. He walked a few more feet before stopping at a large wooden door. "This is your suite."

When he handed identical keys to me and then Ro, I grinned, pounds of anxiety shedding away from me. "I get to stay with Ro?"

"It's not traditional for a woman to share a suite in the men's lodging hall, but apparently Cyrus insisted on you two staying together when he called the school last night. You each have your own bedroom, and will share a living space and bathroom. Usually, first-year students don't get such nice lodgings, but since you are both likely as advanced as the rest of your age group and since Cyrus is here as a favor to my father, he pulled a few strings. I'll come collect you both at eight a.m. Sleep well." With a quick wink in my direction, Eli sauntered off.

Ro shoved me in the shoulder when he caught me staring at Eli's very...firm exit. "Don't go drooling over a boy on your first day. Especially one like that. His type always thinks with the wrong head, if you catch my drift."

"Shut up, jerk. I wasn't. And like you'd know anything about types. We knew like five people back home." I shoved him through the door and my jaw dropped when I got a look at our suite.

The space was bigger than our entire cabin, with all the furnishings made of polished cherry wood. We even had a giant couch and TV in the shared lounge area, and our beds were twice the size of ours back home. It was just as beautiful as every other glimpse of The Guild we'd seen.

"Maybe leaving home won't be so bad, Ro."

❧ 4 ❧
MAX

I woke up around six, no longer able to contain the urge to explore. Ro and I had stayed up later than usual, taking in the beautiful suite until we eventually planted ourselves in front of the TV for a movie marathon—one of our favorite (and only)—pastimes. Still, after brushing my teeth and changing into leggings and a tank, I wasn't surprised to find that Ro had just as much trouble sleeping in as I had. When you were used to waking before the sun each day to train, it became part of your internal clock. Cyrus had whole mantras about birds and worms and sun salutations. It was annoying, but you do anything for long enough and you can turn it into a habit.

"Planning on going for a run too?" I stretched my hamstrings out one at a time, eager to explore the grounds as quickly as possible.

"Yeah, wanted to squeeze one in before Eli swung by. Plus figured we could try and get a peek at the gym before training. It's bound to be way more elaborate than Cy's. This place is ridiculous." Ro finished tying his gym shoes while I prepared a few bottles of water and ran through the rest of my usual pre-workout stretches. I liked to complain when Cyrus was around to hear it, but in all honesty, morning runs were my favorite part of the day. There was something seriously refreshing about pushing your body as far as it was willing to go. Maybe I was a masochist.

As we wound through the halls, I made sure to let Ro lead. He was way better with directions and finding his way around. I got lost in the woods on a weekly basis. And I'd literally lived my entire life in those very woods.

Tracking was a skill I was constantly trying to get better at, but I only seemed to be getting worse. After five minutes of wandering through empty halls, in a path I'd never be able to replicate on my own, we made our way to the front hall.

The grounds were just as beautiful in the morning light, the entire castle surrounded by a lush forest and smaller buildings that likely housed Guild teams and gyms. Did most teams stay here once they graduated? The place was beautiful enough that I wouldn't mind staying around for a few years.

The backdrop of jagged mountains only served to highlight the quiet isolation of The Guild. Even without protective spells, I doubted many humans found their way to this small pocket of civilization. We'd driven miles yesterday without seeing a single car go by. It was like The Guild found a spot off the map somehow.

We started at a brisk jog, but neither of us had the patience to go easy for long. Before we made it a quarter of a mile, we were running at an all-out sprint, each trying to outdo the other. We learned early on in our childhoods that turning exercise into a competition made it feel less like work and encouraged the time to fly by much more quickly. Though when it came to speed, there wasn't much of a competition. I pulled past Ro quickly, laughing as I heard his growl of frustration. There was a clear track for running, but we were used to obstacles, having all of our cardio training in the middle of a forest, so I carved us our own path, hopping around stray buildings, statues, trees, and boulders, until we eventually made our way into some of the denser areas of the surrounding trees.

After half an hour I circled back to find Ro, and we played our own version of stationary tag. It was a game we invented when we were kids, and it was our favorite way to test our strengths against each other. I was much faster, but Ro was better at defensive maneuvering and ridiculously good at predicting my every move, having sparred with me every day for the last eight years. We squared off, each trying to tag the other on the top of the head—an added difficulty for me, since I was so much shorter, that we'd adjusted as I improved at the game.

After ten minutes, neither of us were any closer to tagging the other until Ro landed next to a thick tree. Seeing my opportunity, I sprinted, using the trunk as a springboard to climb up onto Ro's shoulders. Laughing, I dragged my hand through his hair, sure to mess it up as much as I could. It was my sisterly duty. I cringed when I realized how sweaty and gross he was though.

"Point goes to me today, Ro. We should head back and wash up before Eli comes to grab us." I was winded and layered in enough sweat that I was beyond ready for a shower and platter of breakfast foods.

A loud clap interrupted my laughter and Ro spun around, me still swaying awkwardly on his shoulders, and tensed. We were so used to being isolated in our cabin that we weren't accustomed to observers. For a moment, we'd both forgotten we were on new terrain. Running had a way of taking us away from the world for a bit.

"Well done, Max." I recognized Eli's deep, smooth voice.

I hopped down from Ro, a smile still on my face until I noticed who was standing next to Eli.

The surly guy from the dining hall stood a few inches taller than Eli, at well over six feet. His dark hair, stubble, and eyes, added to his mysterious and standoffish aura, and his grim expression had me uncharacteristically annoyed. The dude seemed to just exude anger, which pissed me off. I hadn't done anything to earn it.

Unable to hold eye contact, I looked to the right, finding that they weren't alone. A girl, who seemed to be about the same age as them, stood next to Eli. She had long, shiny black hair that was looped up in a ponytail. Her skin was fair and smooth and looked like she'd never had a single blemish in her entire life, which was infuriating in a weird way. But I was quickly drawn to her eyes. They were the most intense emerald green shade I'd ever seen. Dark full brows that I would kill for made them stand out even more. She studied me with curiosity for a long moment before glancing quickly at Ro.

All three were dressed in black athletic pants and t-shirts that clung tight enough to make it glaringly obvious that they were all stacked with the type of lean muscle that you only got from daily training.

"Max, Ro, these are two of the members of my team." Eli nodded towards Green Eyes first, "this is Declan and this," he gestured quickly to the grumpy one, "is Atlas. He's the team leader."

Ro nodded in greeting, so I followed suit, unsure if my mouth would be able to form words. I didn't expect every single protector I met to be more intimidating than the last.

"Dec, Atlas, you both owe me twenty bucks." Eli winked in my direction, the flirtatious grin I was becoming familiar with planted back on his face. "I bet on you, beautiful."

"You're fast, Max, it'll be fun training with you later. It's always fun when a girl can give the guys around here a run for their money." Declan looked down at me and I found myself gaping at the unfair combination of beautiful eyes and a soft Irish accent. I felt so plain in comparison. My theory on the protectors here getting hit by the pretty stick was looking more and more like a reality.

"I was on my way to grab a quick breakfast before getting you two, do you want to join us instead?" Eli asked. The sun was peeking through a bit, highlighting all of the different shades of brown and amber in his hair.

Ro nodded, and the loud growl coming from my stomach served as my own answer.

"Actually, I'm going to go setup for the morning session, E, I'll catch you guys later." Atlas nodded to Ro, "nice to meet you," and then completely ignored me before turning around and jogging away from us. I gripped my hand into a fist and found myself getting angry. I didn't know what the hell this guy's problem with me was, but I was determined to find out.

I piled two plates full of enough scrambled eggs to keep a dozen chickens busy, along with a stack of bacon and sausage. The unlimited food thing? I could totally get used to this. I turned to Declan, curious about what the first day of training for me and Ro would entail. I found her staring at me with her jaw dropped, not a morsel of food on her plate.

"What?" I asked, shoving a strip of bacon into my mouth before wiping any grease droplets off my chin.

Ro started laughing, before adding a cackled, "trust me, the girl will never be full. She could eat enough to energize half your army and she'd still be able to pack more away."

I swallowed the bacon, and then my embarrassment, noticing that my plate tripled and quadrupled almost everyone else's. "Hey, if we're training all day, I need the energy. This is just smart. Always be prepared, isn't that the protector motto?"

"I think that's the boy scouts, Max." Ro bit back another laugh, cutting his pancake into even, precise bites.

"It's refreshing to see a girl who doesn't eat like a rabbit," Declan said while grabbing a strip of my bacon and earning herself a growl. I didn't share.

With a wink, she took a bite and directed us towards a table in the back, the same one I'd spotted Atlas at last night. It was empty except for one person. He had pale blue eyes made more startlingly bright by the golden-brown hue of his skin and shortly-cropped dark hair. When he noticed us approaching, a brief smirk brightened his face, revealing a cute dimple that made my knees go a little wobbly. As we reached him, Declan pulled out a seat next to her own allowing me to sit. I wasn't used to being around girls, and my nerves at the prospect of making a new friend were making me queasy.

Declan cleared her throat. "Wade, this is Max and Ro. Ro, Max, this is Wade. He's the final, and newest, member of our team."

"You're Cyrus's kids right?" Wade asked, his light blue eyes lingering on me for a long moment with curiosity.

We didn't usually engage in conversation when we ate our meals, so I tried swallowing my obscenely large mouthful of eggs in time to answer, but Ro beat me to the punch.

"Sort of. He kind of took us in when we were younger. We're both adopted."

"That's awesome. My brother's always told me how amazing of a fighter he was. He's a bit of a legend around here." Wade took a giant sip of coffee and I scrunched my nose in jealousy. I'd missed the coffee machine in my first pass through the line. I would have to make sure to hit it on my second.

"Well, to us he's mostly just known as a guy who doesn't believe in sleeping in or rest days." I looked around the dining hall which was beginning to thin out as students and team members went off to start their days. My eyes caught on a gray-haired old man who was swimming in a large lab coat. "Seamus mentioned that The Guild conducts research here. What exactly do you all study?" My brain spun off, wondering if some secret Frankenstein experiment was going on in the basement, under my feet, and if I could find a way to get in on that shit. I freaking loved Mary Shelley. Plus, I wouldn't hate the opportunity to get some up close looks at the creatures we were training to kill.

Wade and Eli shared a grim look before Declan turned to me, her teeth lightly playing with her full bottom lip. "The Guild doesn't always prefer us to take out our targets during assignments. Occasionally, when we have the opportunity, they want us to bring the subjects here to study."

"What are they looking for?" I asked, my eyes drawn to the soft anger coating Wade's expression. It was strange to see his kind, boyish face so stern, like there were two different versions of him suddenly at war.

"We think they are trying to study the origins of their magic. To see if there's any relation to our own history. It's always been decreed that protectors descend from angels, but no one knows if the angels still really exist or, if they do, whether they come from somewhere different than the hell realm." Wade pushed his food around his plate. "Either way, they don't generally share their research with us. It's all very top secret and I'm not totally convinced that they use the most ethical practices."

"Yeah," Eli added, "I don't think my dad even knows what's going on in the basement most of the time. It's all kept very hush hush." He paused a beat. "I'll tell you one thing though, it's not pleasant to be down there. They often force the cleaning on students who've misbehaved."

I cringed, not wanting to know what sort of cleaning had to be done in an eerily mysterious lab that used living subjects. My brain instantly went to Dexter levels of gruesome.

"Why? What's so bad about being down there?" I shoved my tray away, for once in my life no longer hungry.

"There's a lot of dangerous beasts down there that they study. Protectors are generally a fearless bunch, but between the screams from the research and the sheer number of creatures, it's not really the sort of place you want to camp out for a vacation." Declan pushed herself away from the table, her tone an unusual mix of anger and boredom. "I should head out. Need to run by the cabin for my bag before training starts." She turned to me, her lips twitching with the ghost of a smile. "Ro, Max, pleasure. I'll be seeing you both real soon."

"We should probably start walking to the gym, don't want you two to be late on your first day." Eli grabbed my tray, taking it towards the garbage station before circling back with a fresh water bottle. "Here, after your pre-morning workout, hydration is key." With a wink, he and Wade led us back out of the main building and onto the grounds at a slow, leisurely pace.

"So what exactly does our schedule look like today?" I asked, suddenly aware that I had absolutely no idea what our life here would entail. I was used to sparring for several hours with Ro before burying myself in books and online research. Even though we were homeschooled, we'd learned enough to earn us a bachelor degree. Living in a cabin with no other friends or things to do kind of made learning one of the only ways to have fun.

Wade smiled and I found myself once again struck by his boyish beauty, something about him seemed both kind and lethal somehow. "Workouts and sparring practice in the mornings. You will both go to some theory-based classes with your age group later. And if it's decided that private tutoring would be ideal, Arnell and I will tutor you both."

"Arnell?" I asked, only paying partial attention. I'd been inconspicuously scanning the faces we passed as we walked through the campus. It took me a moment to realize that I was looking for Cyrus. "Do you know where Cyrus will be while we train and study?"

"Arnell is from another team. He was from the same year as me." Wade paused. "I'm a bit younger than the rest of the Alpha Six team."

Alpha Six? Was that seriously the kind of naming inspiration this place was bringing for its teams? Boring.

"How old are you guys anyway?" I asked, immediately feeling Ro's elbow in my ribs as soon as the question left my mouth. Right, asking someone's age was rude.

Eli laughed while I rubbed out what would likely be a bruised rib for the next hour. "I'm twenty-three, Wade's twenty-one, and Declan and Atlas are both twenty-four. To answer your other question, Cyrus is probably being reintroduced to the campus and grounds this morning and catching up with my dad. A lot has changed since he was last here. And things have been a bit tense here the last few weeks."

"Why? What's been going on the last few weeks?" I studied Wade and Eli as they glanced at each other, clearly trying to discern how much they could say to us. I opened my mouth to encourage them to spill when a striking man walked up to us.

He had deep brown skin and dark eyes that a girl could melt in. Great, more of that pretty I was talking about. I was going to get a complex living here.

"Eli, Wade," he nodded, "I hear you guys are showing the new recruits around, thought I'd introduce myself before you ruined their lives in training this morning."

"We were just talking about you, Arnell. This is Ro and Max, they arrived with Cyrus last night." Wade paused while we all shook hands, I grinned at the way Arnell's hungry eyes landed on Ro. Apparently turning girls to butter wasn't his style. Ro blushed and I turned back to Wade, urging him to continue. "Oh, um, Arnell is a part of another one of our Alpha teams, here, he does a lot of our tech work. The guy's a genius when it comes to computers. He'll also be working with one or both of you over the next few weeks to get you acclimated to how we do things here. He's a great teacher. If we didn't need him so badly on field work, he'd probably take over several classes in the academy full-time."

Arnell bowed slightly, eyes only for Ro. "Looking forward to working with you both." With a smirk that made even my heart stutter, he turned and walked back towards the building.

"You're drooling, Ro," I whispered, flicking his chin with my finger. I wasn't above teasing him about it after he'd called me out for admiring Eli last night.

He lightly shoved me in retaliation, landing me in a pocket of mud. I flung my now filthy arm in his direction, pleased when the dirt splattered across his white shirt.

"Oh, you two are going to be fun." Eli smiled, stepping forward and opening a door to a large building. The architecture was much more modern than the castle, and it looked like it was styled roughly as an athletic stadium. "We're here, try not to die."

❧ 5 ❧
MAX

The gym was huge, the stadium opening up into a giant floor plan filled with large blue sparring mats. The walls were all covered with various training weapons: wooden swords with dulled blades, staffs, and even real blades for throwing practice. The circular room was also lined with doors, which I guessed led to smaller, more intimate or specialized training rooms, and judging by the steam billowing beneath one of the doors, a large bathroom for cleaning up after training sessions. The idea of having a real, proper gym to train in was wild.

How had Cyrus given all of this up for so many years? And why did he want us to miss out on the opportunity to train with the best as soon as possible?

Annoyingly, my gaze almost instantly found Atlas, and I watched in guilty fascination as he and Declan sparred; they moved with impressive grace, like their fight was more of a dance, even though their smiles and laughs made it clear that they weren't investing all of their energy into their actions. For a moment, their carefree battle and clear trust reminded me of Ro and all of our fights growing up. Sometimes, when training was how you spent your life, you had to learn to find fun in it. Maybe we would fit in here better than I'd originally thought.

We weren't like regular people, but maybe we were like these people.

A small group of girls my age, maybe a little bit older, sat watching the battle—in particular Atlas—with adoration. I wondered, briefly if they were together, one of those bonded pairs that Eli mentioned last night. They seemed to anticipate each other's every move, like they were two parts of a whole. They were completely oblivious to the gathered audience, lost instead in the movement.

I was definitely rooting for Declan, but each time I thought she'd gained the edge, Atlas shifted unexpectedly and she was back at ground zero.

Wade mumbled something about them being show-offs and led me and Ro to the large group of students. Judging by their appearance, I guessed they were all close to our age group, more or less. None looked older than twenty. Eli was right though, the men outnumbered the women significantly, and I counted only six femme-presenting people in the mass of at least fifty bodies. I wasn't sure if there really were so few female protectors or if The Guild just didn't accept them here as frequently as they did males.

Eli catcalled, drawing Declan's embarrassed attention, and they both stopped battling. Their surprised expressions made it clear that they weren't aware they had an audience.

"Looks like everyone is here early to see the new recruits," Eli whispered, goosebumps trailing down my neck from the feel of his breath along the shell of my ear. He wasn't even standing that close to me, but I was aware of him with every fiber of my body.

"Everyone's here, so no use waiting. Let's get started now," Atlas said, as he glanced around the room. He and Declan moved through the crowd, pairing everyone up. My heart dropped slightly when Atlas pulled Ro towards a larger man across the room.

I'd never sparred with anyone other than Ro or Cyrus, and throwing my fist at someone seemed like an odd way to introduce myself or make new friends. Not that I had a whole lot of experience in the friendship department, so for all I knew, a fist in the face of a protector was like a hug to a human. Here's hoping.

Declan walked up to me, and my eyes were drawn to the fascinating designs tattooed along her arms. "Max, I'm going to pair you with Reza, I think you two will be a good fit for sparring. She's one of our best fighters in The Guild, amongst both students and teams. It'll be fun to see how you two match up."

A girl my build, but a few inches taller, walked up to us. She had beautiful blond hair wrapped back in an elaborate braided ponytail and dark blue eyes. I extended my hand for an introduction, excited by the prospect of making a new friend. Her gaze edged towards my offered hand and a disgusted grimace took over her otherwise pretty features. "You'll get no special treatment from me, princess, just because you've trained with Cyrus and are the campus's shiny new toy."

"Er, right. Nice to meet you, too." I guess that friendship goal was a little presumptuous, then.

Declan walked off shaking her head, the echo of her lilting chuckle amplifying my already frayed nerves.

I watched as the other pairs squared off and began to spar, trying to get a feel for the fighting strategies they used here. Slowly, younger students and older protectors stumbled into the gym area, some veering off into the smaller rooms, others hopping into battle across the gym. I turned my attention back towards my class. There didn't seem to be a signal, everyone just started fighting at once.

Which meant that I wasn't totally paying attention to Reza and didn't get the memo that she wanted to start until I felt her fist colliding with my jaw. Apparently there was no formal bowing here or even a chipper whistle to tell us to 'go.'

Luckily, she made a breath of noise as she moved, so my reflexes had me leaning slightly to the right to avoid most of the impact. I turned my attention back to her, studying the placement of her feet, her hands, her shoulders. The first few punches were easy to deflect, as her eyes traveled towards her goal well before her body followed. And if anything, her added height would only benefit me—I was used to sparring with men who had bulk and inches on me.

I remained on the defensive, studying, trying to soak in as much information about her style and approach as I could. One of Cyrus's first rules was to learn as much about your enemy as possible—knowledge won battles long before brawn, as far as he was concerned.

Getting frustrated with my evasions, Reza pounced, announcing her arrival with a loud grunt before she made contact. I stepped slightly to the side and, using her momentum, flipped her over me, landing her flat on her back. Her frustrated growl signaled that she was growing annoyed with our fight. I wasn't as easy of an opponent as she'd planned, and now her heightened frustration would only make her sloppy. Did they not teach the students to mask their emotions in this place?

Calmness and clarity were two of Cyrus's staples. He'd been ramming them into me for as long as I could remember, so I'd assumed it was a protector thing. While most toddlers learned how to color inside the lines and play well with others, I was learning how to meditate as Cyrus deliberately tried to distract me. It was one of his favorite games. The guy had a sick sense of fun.

After a few minutes, during which Reza's efforts met with the same result, Declan called time. I turned, realizing that everyone's eyes were on us, both our peers and the professional teams filtering in around the perimeter—the awareness of which seemed to heighten Reza's embarrassment and solidify her hatred of me.

I let out a sigh. Maybe the quickest way to make friends would be throwing my fights?

I looked over at Ro and noticed a nice red welt lightly coloring his cheek and smirked. He was at a bit more of a disadvantage than I was. While I was used to fighting partners larger than me, he was used to the opposite. It looked like his current match was exactly that—a match.

"Theo, come here. I want you to try pairing up with Max. Reza, you can go back to fighting Izzy." Declan motioned me over towards Theo. Reza stormed across the room in a hurry, but not before shooting me a glare that had me feeling guilty, though I wasn't really sure why.

Theo was a couple of inches taller than me, but shorter than most of the other guys in the room. That said, he was bulky with hard muscle, and had at least fifty or sixty pounds on me. He gave my body a quick scan that had my skin crawling and then chuckled like he wasn't impressed with what he found. I smiled, showing teeth—this was more like it. Fighting him would be fun.

As soon as Eli called time, Theo charged. He was stronger than me, but his steps were hard and clunky, easy for me to evade. Using his weight against him, I leveraged my shoulder into his waistline, flipping him easily to the mat. In some ways, Reza was the better opponent. She announced her moves a lot of the time, but they were still good moves. Theo fought like he was throwing spaghetti at a wall, just hoping something would stick.

His next attempt was met with an even harder thump to the ground, his male pride becoming as much of a hindrance to his style as his heavy movements. A large, meaty fist came barrelling towards my face. At the last moment, I ducked, using my left foot to sweep his legs.

Theo's face burned red with embarrassed frustration as he fell back again, bouncing slightly on the rubbery mat. Anger radiated off him in droves so strong I was afraid I'd get burnt. The lack of female protectors here made the men complacent, set in their archaic beliefs that men were the superior fighters. He thought it was a weakness, to lose to a girl. A better fighter would realize that I was simply well versed in the sport, a worthy adversary. Ro never acted like I'd attacked his masculinity on occasions when I beat him.

While Theo gathered his ego on the floor, Atlas dragged Wade over to our fighting space. "Bentley, you'll spar with Wade."

My body froze. Bentley.

It seemed that Cyrus had given us his last name when he enrolled us here. We'd never had need for a surname before, and my belly warmed with the strange connection that gave us; he was claiming us as his, we were family. I knew we were family, of course, Ro and Cyrus were all I had. But Cyrus wasn't the mushy sentimental sort, so this was unexpected.

Theo charged off the mat, swearing softly until Atlas shot him a glare, effectively shutting him up. While he didn't respect me, it was clear that he respected, even feared, Atlas. Wade stood in front of me, his posture alerting me instantly to the fact that he was a far better fighter than my previous two contenders. When he watched me, it wasn't with the expectation that he would win. He seemed to view me as an equal of sorts, like he was intrigued to see how my style would react with his.

Atlas stood at the edge of the mat, ready to observe, a realization that caused an unfamiliar nervousness to coat my muscles. I didn't want to lose, sure. But the thought of losing while he witnessed it, had my blood heating to uncomfortable levels.

Wade rolled his neck from side to side, offering a shy smile my way. When Atlas signaled the start of our match, Wade remained still, waiting for me to attack. He studied me intensely, like I was a science experiment and he was waiting for some unusual reaction to occur. I shivered slightly, uncomfortable with the attention and perusal. Neither of us moved for what felt like an eternity. It seemed that, like Theo, he wasn't used to fighting against a girl, at least not one of my size. Though, unlike Theo, his hesitation seemed to be buried more in a fear of hurting me than fear for his own ego.

Well, I'd fix that quickly. I wasn't a delicate flower and I most definitely didn't want to be treated like one either.

I charged, feigning right before taking aim with my left fist. Wade was faster than Reza and Theo, and much better at reading his opponent. He ducked, but not quickly enough: my fist pressed lightly into his shoulder before I circled back and planted a foot into his right kidney. He landed on his knees with a whimper. Kidney hits hurt like a bitch, and I was mildly sorry since Wade seemed like a nice enough guy. But Cyrus taught me never to show mercy, not even towards him and Ro. We got extra laps if he thought we were going too easy on each other.

I grinned at Wade, encouraging him to go on the offensive. He was fast and smart, able to hide most of his intentions. I could see why he made one of the best teams so young. Still, after ten minutes, only two of his hits landed, and when they did they were too soft. He was holding back, the knowledge of which fueled my frustration.

When Ro took it easy on me, it was an insult, not a favor. It was something he'd only do when he was trying to piss me off. Usually, we were equals. Happy to give as good as we got.

I lashed out, landing a hard kick into Wade's abdomen before tackling him to the ground. I straddled his waist, my knees pinning him in place as I struck him with a few hits to the chest, hard enough to make him bruise but not cause any significant damage. His light blue eyes darkened, his hands making their way to my hips, holding me there but not resisting my attack. What kind of battle strategy was this place teaching these boys? No wonder they needed Cyrus here. The heat from his hands and his eyes had me pulling my attention away from the fight. I stopped swatting at his chest, staring down at him in confusion.

The left side of his lips quirked up in a grin and he gave my waist a soft squeeze that made me squirm, before flipping me to the mat and reversing our positions.

That...was not a strategy I was familiar with. I swallowed, trying desperately to dislodge the flutters rolling around in my abdomen. Being pinned underneath him like this was so much more intense and intimate than kissing Michael had been.

"Enough." Atlas nudged Wade off of me, then pulled me up by the shoulders, lifting me off the mat, his grip hard enough to bruise. "You held back intentionally, Wade. This isn't a place to flirt. Not taking this seriously is how lives are lost."

Wade's nostrils flared and I watched as his eyes stared daggers into Atlas's. They seemed to be in a silent war of wills, until eventually Wade looked away first.

Embarrassed, I ripped myself from Atlas's grasp, looking out at the rest of the room. Almost everyone had stopped sparring to watch us. Except for Ro. He was currently pummeling his partner, apparently not needing more than a few minutes to adjust to fighting a new body type. He seemed to be having a lot more fun right now than I was, that's for sure.

"From now on, Ro and Max spar only with someone from our team," Atlas said, still avoiding eye contact with me. "Wade, you're done for the day. If you can figure out how to fight her like an equal, you can join in again tomorrow."

While Atlas was glaring at me like I was the embodiment of evil, and while I felt sorry for Wade's clear frustration, it was nice that he was enforcing the fighting experience I needed. I wanted to improve and quickly. I hadn't grown up around protectors other than Cyrus and Ro, and I didn't want to be left behind or coddled. The werewolf attack was a rude awakening. The creatures I'd be expected to kill or capture were so much stronger than I was. And I was pretty damn good already, if I was honest with myself. So if I wanted to stand a chance, I needed to be great.

For the rest of the morning, and well into the afternoon, I

fought with Declan and Eli, sometimes both at once, shifting back and forth between hand-to-hand combat and using wooden staffs. After a few hours, I was drenched in an unattractive layer of sweat—both of my partners more than giving me a run for my money. I could take Eli more than half the time when we were just sparring, but his skills with the staff far outdid my own. I wasn't nearly as good with weapons as I was without them, something that frustrated Cy to no end.

And while Declan was quite a bit taller and curvier than me, which should have slowed her down, her moves were unpredictable and hard to defend against. I couldn't get into her headspace the way I could with everyone else I'd fought. Atlas kept poor Ro busy for the rest of the morning, and from the purple and green shades pebbling his skin, I knew that Ro was on the losing end of most, if not all of those battles.

When Atlas called time for the day, I collapsed onto the mat, chest lifting up and down in hard, heavy breaths. It was a good feeling—I always loved the exhaustion that sunk into my bones after a particularly good training session. And today, I got to spar with four new people, so my mind and body were stretched more tightly than I was used to. It was great.

A small girl with short brown hair, warm olive skin, and gray eyes bent over me, offering her hand. She pulled me up with more strength than I would've given her credit for. I guess I also needed to toss out my assumptions and biases. Her skin was slick with sweat, but it somehow made her look like she was glowing, not grossly in need of a long shower.

"Thanks," I mumbled, my breath coming out awkward spurts from the workout. She was taller than me, but where most of the people here towered over me, she was only a couple of inches out of my range.

"That was impressive today." She paused a beat, before quietly adding, "and I particularly loved watching you kick the shit out of Reza and my brother."

My mouth fell open slightly, probably making me look like a

fish. "Theo's your brother?" I catalogued her dark hair and shorter frame. Knowing they were related, I could see the resemblance, but this girl definitely made it out of the womb with the better personality. And I'd only heard her utter one sentence.

"Unfortunately. Not that he likes to admit we're related," she laughed. "He's an ass, but he has his moments. Like all brothers, I suppose."

Her smile was warm, friendly, and infectious, automatically inspiring one of my own.

"I'm Izzy. It'll be nice to have another girl around here, Max." Her hand clasped mine in a firm but amicable shake.

Maybe beating people up *was* the way to find friends here after all.

"Hey listen, there's a get together tonight if you want to come? I imagine being new here is probably overwhelming, so it might be a good way for you to meet some people outside of gym time. Your brother's welcome too, of course. The more tolerable people I can con into showing up, the better. It's Theo's birthday. And I'm sort of required to show up." She tossed me her water bottle and I drained half of it instantly, feeling slightly bad for beating him up on his birthday.

"That would be really great," I said, trying not to stumble over my words in my excitement. "I've never been to a birthday party before."

Izzy frowned slightly, studying me until I broke eye contact, embarrassed by the revelation.

"Really? That's cool, it'll be an even more fun experience then." She smiled again, revealing bright, straight teeth, and I exhaled, relaxing a bit. "I was thinking of going to the mall later to buy something to wear. One of the guys who carried your stuff up last night mentioned that you didn't bring too much with you, so you're welcome to join me. And I'm guessing none of the boys mentioned it yet, but when you're part of The Guild, you get a pretty hefty expense account." She winked conspiratorially. "You should see my shoe collection. It's my pride and joy."

An actual trip to the mall? With a friend who wasn't Ro?

"That'd be fantastic." My voice cracked with excitement. "I just have to check in with Cyrus before leaving. I'm not really sure how things work here yet, or how comfortable he'll be with me leaving on my first day." But oh man was I willing to put him through the world's largest guilt trip if he didn't let me go.

Eli walked up, laughing as he collected a few stray wooden staffs from the session. "Who knew that a girl who fought like you do would be interested in a shopping spree?"

"Hey." I shoved him playfully in the arm, but hard enough to cause him to stumble slightly. "Just because I know how to kick ass, doesn't mean I'm not also allowed to like shoe shopping. It's not an either or kind of situation. Women aren't monoliths."

"Hell yes," Izzy said, her voice sing-songy, "I knew I liked you." She grabbed her gym bag before threading her arm through mine. "Let's get lunch. I could eat an entire cow right now."

⁂

THE AFTERNOON THEORY CLASS WAS INTERESTING, BUT ALMOST impossible for me to follow. Judging by Ro's blank face and the doodles he etched into his notebook, he'd felt the same. I never realized just how basic our understanding of our own history really was. And I was starting to seriously question Cyrus's reasons for keeping us in the dark.

Not to mention that it was hard to come into the middle of a lesson, in the middle of the year, and take anything worthwhile from the hour-long session. Especially since so much of the lesson focused on specific surveillance techniques and discussions of various supernatural battle strategies. Not to mention the fact that Ro and I weren't used to learning in a traditional classroom. It felt like we'd been plopped down in the middle of a new world with no primers.

Confusion aside though, I was eager to learn everything that I possibly could. And I hoped that we could still take Arnell and Wade up on their offer of extra lessons.

The instructor was young, maybe in her early thirties. But I guess most protectors were young here. I'd only seen a few walking the grounds who appeared any older than fifty. She had long black hair and a no bullshit attitude about her which I liked instantly.

"Typically," she paced back and forth at the front of the room, her shoes making a weirdly comforting click-clack sort of sound, "you will be placed in a team that can use your specific talents. The Guild works to create balanced teams that are best able to utilize each protector's strengths. As you know, we study you intensely throughout your schooling, so that when the time comes to join your team—or," she paused, her crystal-blue eyes meeting mine briefly, "potential bondmates, you will be positioned for success."

Bondmates again. I repressed a shiver and glanced over at Ro. He was studying her with rapt attention, taking diligent notes. I wasn't surprised. He had that model student air about him.

I raised my hand, drawing the attention of everyone in the class.

"Yes, Ms. Bentley." She tilted her head to the side, studying me like a cat. Her voice was crisp, but not unfriendly.

I cleared my throat, all too aware of the attention lasering in on me. Izzy was next to me and I felt her squeeze my hand gently, offering some much needed encouragement. "Er, Ms. sorry—:"

"Everyone calls me Reese," she said, arching a brow to encourage me to continue.

"Right, Ms., er, Reese. Are we given no choice about which teams we work with or who we bond to?"

A soft, almost imperceptible smile lit her features. "The Guild does try to take into consideration your choice, yes. But the success of the unit as a whole is of utmost importance. The stakes are too high to place too much attention on individual whims."

I sank back into my chair, highly aware of the tension running through Ro on my left. He was thinking the same thing I was: there was no fucking way we'd be joining separate teams. There was one person I trusted to have my back at every obstacle, and it was him. So we'd either need to prove to everyone that we worked best together, or else we'd have to consider going out on our own when the time came.

Reese turned, ready to continue her lecture, but I wasn't done. "Sorry, but what if we don't want to bond?"

I felt more than saw Izzy's head whip in my direction, and several heavy intakes of breath sounded around the room. Slowly, Reese turned around, once again pinning me with her bright, intelligent eyes.

"Bondmates are a long, time-honored tradition, Ms. Bentley. If Guild leaders feel you are valuable enough to pair up, it is not something you turn down. Again, the stakes in our world are high."

"Isn't it, I don't know, a little creepy though? Being forced to bind your life to someone else? Kind of arranged-marriage-like, don't you think?"

Her face drained of emotion as she scanned the rest of the class, assessing before responding. "You grew up around humans, Max. It's to be expected that our customs and traditions seem odd to you." She walked a few steps closer to where I was sitting in the first row. "I can assure you that the relationship I shared with my own bondmate was one of the most rewarding experiences of my life. We were a team, even closer than—" she broke off, her eyes glistening a bit as she cleared her throat. "You'll learn, as you come to understand our world, you'll come to understand the nature of bond ceremonies. They serve an important purpose."

I wasn't sold, but I also didn't want to upset her, so I simply nodded and sat back in my desk, pen poised over paper. The rest of the lesson was uneventful as she walked through various techniques different teams used, while going over old field missions as examples for us to learn from.

At dinner, we found Cyrus sitting at a table with Seamus, the rest of the hall's eyes trying to inconspicuously study the man who was apparently a legend to these people. I wondered what they'd think of him if they saw him wandering around the cabin wearing boxers and a beat up Seinfeld t-shirt while making his way through a six-pack of beer. He wasn't exactly a Clark Kent figure when he was off the job. He was just Cyrus.

"Can we go to the mall and a party tonight, Cy?" I looked up, blushing at the soft snickering from the next table over. It must have seemed strange to these people that I asked permission. Yes, I was eighteen, but Ro and I were used to respecting Cyrus and he was used to keeping us on a tight leash. Something about living in paranoid isolation in the middle of the mountains did that to a guy. And well, he had his faults, but he did his best to be a father figure to us and we had no problem seeking his approval or advice. He'd more than earned our respect over the years.

His eyes flashed briefly to the mocking glances and when he turned back to me he nodded, his eyes pinched slightly.

"Here." His voice was gruff, but I could tell amusement was hiding behind it as he slid over a phone and credit card to each of us. "These are yours now that you're officially considered a part of The Guild. Your account will go up if and when you become a member of a team."

Something about the way he said that made me think he planned on getting us out of here long before Ro and I had a chance to join a team in any official capacity. Which was a bummer, I kind of wanted a life purpose and a clear path to obtain it. The Guild offered that. Why did he work so hard to shield us from this life?

"You're both going to this gathering, correct?" Cyrus's eyes traveled back and forth between us as we nodded. "Still, I'd be more comfortable if you left the grounds with someone more suited to protection. You two get into more trouble than you're worth."

"I'll go with them." Eli pulled a chair up next to me, dropping his overflowing tray onto the table. Without saying another word, he grabbed a large piece of pizza and dropped it on my now empty plate.

"Thanks," I mumbled, my mouth watering.

"You earned it. Now I know why you eat so freaking much. I haven't seen someone expend that much energy on a single sparring session in, well, maybe ever."

I grinned behind a mouthful. At first, I was a little put off by his overt flirtation, but anyone who brought me food was okay in my book. This was the start of a beautiful friendship.

Wade walked up, dragging another chair with him. He shoved Eli over and sat down between us. "Yeah, she's small but mighty. You guys going to Theo's party later on?" He asked, grabbing a handful of fries off of Eli's plate and eyeing my crust.

"Don't even think about it," I said, grabbing the crust before he got any ideas. "I don't share food."

He smirked but withdrew his hand immediately. "Wouldn't dream of it." Wade looked over at Cyrus and Seamus. "I heard the first day of class was a bit overwhelming, so if it's alright with you both, I think Arnell and I should start additional tutoring sessions soon, to get Max and Rowan caught up as quickly as possible."

How did he know that Ro and I were basically lost during most of our classes? Aside from my obvious skepticism about teams and bonds, I thought we'd done a decent job of pretending to understand everything.

Cyrus looked grim. I imagined the idea of us learning more about the protector world didn't settle well with him. There was a reason he'd kept us bunkered in the woods for eighteen years. We just didn't know what it was.

While he'd taught us the basics: *vampires and werewolves, bad; knife to the heart and decapitation, good*, he wasn't fond of discussing the world in detail. Especially when it came to magic or the unexplainable. I had no idea what made him leave the world in the first place, and was just as clueless about what made him suddenly want to return to it. Mysteries didn't sit well with me, so I was determined to unpack this one eventually.

"Fine," he mumbled, sipping his drink which smelled way too strong to just be a soda. I wasn't sure what the rules at The Guild were, but hopefully Cyrus wouldn't get fired just yet—I was having way too much fun and it was only my first day. Who knew what else this place would bring?

"I'm also available for any extra sessions too," Eli said, face splitting into a mischievous grin. "For the record, I was a top student and excellent tutor, so feel free to take advantage of me." He whispered the last part so quietly that I barely caught it.

Cyrus studied Wade and Eli, every muscle in his body tensed and still. There was something unfamiliar in his eyes that I hadn't seen before. If I had to put a label on it, I'd call it...fear.

❧ 6 ☙
WADE

I pushed into the cabin, my brain buzzing with frustration. After quickly tossing my keys onto the table and kicking off my shoes, I took the stairs three at a time before busting into the team office, not even bothering to knock. I knew that only Atlas would be around.

"What the hell, man," I said, trying and failing to keep the heat out of my words, "why the hell were you such an asshole today? That was totally uncalled for."

I wasn't used to Atlas calling me out in front of other people, and today he went way too far.

He was leaning forward in his usual chair, his head bowed over the notebooks scattered across the desk. His muscles were tense and after a couple of deep breaths, he turned and met my eyes, his fingers pinching the bridge of his nose in frustration.

Good, I was frustrated too.

"You were going easy on the girl. I was just stating the obvious, Wade. I can't always coddle you." He scratched the scruff lining his cheek, turning back towards his notebook, like that was the end of the conversation.

I clenched my jaw before walking further into the room. I was not going to be dismissed so easily. I was a part of this team, and it was about damn time that Atlas stopped treating me like a kid. Gripping the corner of his chair, I pulled, spinning it around just enough that he was facing me again. "It was her first day, and that's not even what I meant. Your comment about getting her killed. Do you—" I dropped down into the chair across from him, sinking down into the buried guilt. "Is that what you really think? Do you think I got Sarah killed? For not pushing her hard enough?"

It was the thing that had plagued my nightmares—watching her get taken down by three werewolves while Atlas and I tried to hold the rest of the pack back. I blamed myself, but it cut deep to know that Atlas did too.

His face instantly softened, his dark eyes filling with concern. It was rare for him to show anything like affection to most people, but he was empathetic with his team. "No, Wade." He groaned, running his hands through his hair roughly. It was one of his nervous ticks, one of the only things he did that revealed what was going through his mind. "What happened to Sarah, that wasn't your fault. That was on both of us. She had bad intel, and we were overrun. We—you did everything you could. I know that. And you need to stop blaming yourself for what happened. We didn't stand a chance. We're lucky that we made it out alive as it is."

His hand gripped my forearm tightly, drawing my eyes back to his. I cleared my throat, trying desperately to push the guilt down. But instead of disappearing, it sank into the pit of my stomach like a heavy boulder. "We should've protected her. It's what bonded pairs do. We let her down." My voice broke slightly, and I hated myself for it. I could usually keep my emotions in check, but not about this and not around Atlas. He could read me too well, so there was no point in even trying.

Atlas's jaw tightened before breaking eye contact. He had been against the bond from the start, and only eventually agreed to it because it was the only way he could get good old dad, Tarren, to let us stay at the North American Guild Headquarters, with the rest of our team. Usually protectors didn't force their children to bond with a female until their mid-to-late twenties, if at all, but Sarah was well connected and so Tarren didn't give Atlas much of a choice.

"The bond never fully took." His voice was soft, and I listened with every fiber of my being. He never talked about it, and I didn't want to miss a single syllable. "And honestly Wade, it doesn't matter anymore. They won't force another one on us again for a few years—hell, maybe ever, if we can get away with it. We've done our duty in that department, now we can just focus on our job for the time being—hunting down as many of these fucking killers as we can."

Atlas hated forced protector bonds and had since we were kids. Part of me wondered if he was happy that Sarah was out of the picture now. He'd always called the set up a sham and hated daddy dearest even more than he used to since Tarren had pushed it on him. I shook my head, clearing the thought away almost as quickly as it entered my mind.

Even if Atlas didn't feel as connected to Sarah as I had, he would never let anything happen to anyone under his protection, especially not someone he'd taken an oath to protect with his life. While being bonded to Sarah had given me a feeling of purpose, like I had something to direct my energy towards, it had only ever made Atlas feel shackled. But even so, losing her broke something in him.

Atlas didn't fail, not ever. Until he did. And that night had changed him in more ways than we were prepared for at the time. He was even harder to read than he was before, his focus wrapped so intensely around work that I was sure he would eventually crack open from the pressure.

Self-loathing was a bitch.

"You know that's not true, right? Dad—Tarren, will make sure you bond again and probably pretty soon. Especially if the bond to Sarah, as you claim, wasn't complete. He'll use that. He'll exploit every opportunity he has to solidify his position and your ability to carry out his legacy." I couldn't hide the disgust in my voice. I wasn't jealous of Atlas, nor of the fact that Tarren was far more invested in his future than in mine. If anything, I felt bad for Atlas. As long as I wasn't the favorite, I had more freedom, more choice. Atlas—he was just stuck.

He didn't respond, choosing instead to stare at his lap, lost in his own thoughts. Would I bond again, if given the chance? If it meant that I could stay here, with Atlas and the rest of the team?

I thought back to Max, and the way that I'd been naturally drawn to her since seeing her in the cafeteria earlier. There was attraction, yeah. I mean, anyone with eyes could see that she was beautiful. Everything from her dark black hair and eyes to her full pink lips made it abundantly clear that she was gorgeous. And there was something strangely compelling about the fact she could be such a ferocious fighter, while remaining so incredibly naive and innocent. She was filled with so much curiosity and trust, an open book in some ways, but an absolute mystery in others. It was an odd combination for a protector of her fighting caliber.

But there was something else there, a pull that reminded me of Sarah. Only, where the bond between Sarah and I had been constructed, glued together by magic, my pull to Max felt different somehow—more effortless. More *right*.

"Cyrus's kids...what do you know about them?" I met Atlas's dark gaze again, but his thoughts were just as impenetrable as usual. One thing that was clear though: he was badly in need of a shave and a solid week's worth of sleep. Red was starting to take over the whites of his eyes and he was even more surly than usual, which was a pretty difficult thing to achieve. "Jesus, Atlas, when's the last time you slept? You've been off all week."

I considered throwing a jab about how insomnia could lead to distraction and to getting people killed, especially after the way he called me out today. But I reigned it in at the last second.

He didn't seem like he was in the mood and I didn't want to push him.

Atlas cleared his throat and stretched his head from side to side, relaxing slightly after a few cracks echoed in the room. "I'm fine. Leave Cyrus's kids alone, Wade. We have enough to worry about now with increased attacks. I don't need you mooning over some fresh meat."

I could feel my cheeks heating. Had my attraction to Max really been that obvious? "What do you know about them?" I pressed, ignoring his clear desire to change the subject, yet again. What a surprise, the guy never liked to discuss anything outside of work and duty these days.

"Not much, no one really does," he said, shrugging but not meeting my eyes. "Never heard of them until yesterday and now they're here. That's it. Far as I can tell, Eli didn't know much either beyond the fact that they existed. Which means either Cyrus kept the details about them hidden even from his brother, or Seamus didn't think they were worth mentioning." His mouth dipped into a small frown.

Atlas hated being in the dark and the Bentley family's arrival had shocked everyone. Cyrus had been gone for so long that most of the protector world assumed he was dead. That, or that he was some phantom-like figure built into protector mythology to make us fight harder, be stronger. If we didn't work so closely with Seamus, I'd probably buy into the myth part more than I did.

"They fight well," I said, thinking back to the way that Max had taken me down almost instantly. Yeah, I had been too busy trying to parse through whatever thrall she had over me, the way my skin seemed to hum as I got close to her, but still. There weren't many fighters who could take one of us down like that, especially one as small as her. We weren't on one of the top teams without reason. And Atlas knew it too, or else he wouldn't have announced that we were taking over their sparring matches.

"They're okay," he shrugged, waving me off. "You were going

easy on her. Like I said, you need to be focusing with the right head."

"Dick," I muttered. Maybe he was right. Maybe Max was just fresh meat. The protector community was small enough that most of us grew up knowing each other—hell, half of our matches were determined while we were children. It was a fun pastime for parents, to speculate who would end up bonded to whom. So I guess it wasn't completely impossible that the newness of Max heightened my reaction to her.

Even still, a girl hadn't really caught my attention like that, well, ever. I opened my mouth again before Atlas cut me off with a shake of his head.

"I mean it, Wade. Stay away from her, something about them doesn't feel right. I don't know what it is, but I'll figure it out eventually." Atlas looked back down at his stack of notebooks, no doubt studying all of the wolf hunting patterns that he'd been obsessing over for months. We all wanted revenge for Sarah, but Atlas was consumed by his need for it.

Not willing to be silenced, I threw a pencil at him, forcing him to meet my eyes again. "What do you mean something doesn't feel right? Do you feel the pull too?"

Atlas paled, the blood draining from his face like he'd seen a ghost. "No, don't be ridiculous." He took a long, steady breath in and out before shaking his head. "That kind of magic doesn't exist anymore."

"I know there haven't been any natural bonds forged in ages, but I swear there's something about her, man," I pressed. I watched as Atlas stared, like he was almost looking through me, his face ashen. It was rare for him to be at a loss for words. I sat up straighter, studying him. "You feel it too, don't you?"

Atlas shook his head, jumping back to the present, his characteristic scowl back on his face. "Don't be ridiculous, Wade."

I narrowed my eyes and took a breath in, ready to fight him on this.

"I mean it, Wade, drop it," he barked. "Any connection you

feel is probably born out of a need to get your dick wet. So go do just that if you need to, but leave the girl alone."

With that, he stood up and opened the door, a clear signal for me to leave. Atlas wasn't usually so crass or dismissive, not when it came to me. The fact that he was being so reactive, just amplified my own frustration.

"You can't just order me around, asshole. Besides, I'm going to be tutoring her."

"Fine," he started, stopping his perusal of whichever document was currently in front of him again. "Tutor her, but that's it. We don't need the Bentleys sniffing around in our business. And whatever spell she has over you—you know how bonds work. They can be severed as quickly as they can be enforced. You have enough to work on without getting distracted by some pretty face. Especially if you want to stay on our team. We don't have room or time for dead weight. The stakes are too high."

I fell back deeper into my chair. It felt like I'd been slapped. Atlas had been frustrated with me before, sure. But he'd never threatened to kick me off the team before. Especially not after he'd fought so hard to keep us together and get me my spot here in the first place. Without another word, I stood and left, slamming the door closed as forcefully as I'd opened it.

7

MAX

Every shade of yellow, orange, and red rushed by my window as Izzy drove me, Eli, and Ro into town. Her van gave me some serious soccer mom vibes, but she blasted her pop music loud enough to break the image. It felt so strange, leaving The Guild with two new friends, on our way to a completely normal shopping trip. For a moment, frustration settled in my bones that Cyrus had kept this life, these sorts of normal experiences from us. But I pushed the unease away as quickly as I could. He had his reasons, and I was happy enough to be given the opportunity now. Who knows how long Ro and I would've been locked away if Cyrus hadn't received that letter. I owed Seamus a seriously giant thank you gift.

When we pulled up to the mall, Ro wandered off, mumbling something about not wanting to shop. I followed his line of sight and found Arnell near the food court. I smiled to myself, wondering how long it would take for those two to become a thing. I couldn't wait to give Arnell the protective-older-sister spiel that I'd been planning for years. It didn't matter that I was technically younger than Ro. I had the intimidation thing down to a T.

Izzy steered us immediately to a small boutique shop filled with more dresses and shoes than I'd ever seen.

"Are you guys going to model for me? Because I totally vote that you model for me." Eli ran his hand along a black silk dress sitting on a headless mannequin. "And this should definitely be option number one."

A pretty woman walked up to us, asking us briefly if we needed help finding anything, and then immediately proceeded to ignore us, instead focusing her attention on flirting with Eli. His rakish smile made it abundantly clear that he didn't mind the distraction. Which, honestly, seemed pretty on-brand for him, even though I'd only known him for a day. Izzy rolled her eyes and grabbed my hand, pulling me roughly through the store as she wove around displays, studying some with indifference, some with measured interest.

"Better this way," she said, swiping hangers roughly along the metal racks. "Shopping with men will only slow us down." She grabbed four dresses, guessing at my size and piled them into my arms before shoving me into a closet-sized dressing room. I stared in disgust at the splotches of dried gum on the floor, afraid to take my shoes off to change. I ordered most of my clothes online, and even then they were only basics for fighting, so this wasn't part of my usual shopping process. And the materials and colors that Izzy had picked out? They were nothing like what I was used to wearing.

"Do I really need to try all of these on?" I asked, pawing a black dress with beads and lace. It was pretty, but it didn't seem very pragmatic.

"Yup, and I need to see each one, so no cheating." Her voice rang clear from the dressing room beside mine as I pulled on a strappy red dress first. "So, Max, what was it like growing up outside of the protector community?" She whispered the word 'protector' so that if any other shoppers wandered by, they wouldn't hear. Though I'm sure most humans wouldn't bat an eye if they did. They'd probably assume we were discussing body guards or something.

I laughed, stepping out to show her the dress and glowing with her approving smile.

The material hugged my curves, but was still breathable. It was odd to be wearing something so feminine. I kind of loved it.

After walking back into the crusty dressing room, I peeled the red dress off and tried on a deep sage one that clung to me more tightly than I was comfortable with. "We didn't really grow up around humans either, to be honest. It was just me, Ro, and Cyrus. In a cabin. In the middle of nowhere. Come to think of it, I was practically raised by wolves." And with Cyrus's gruff nature, 'wolves' was possibly putting it lightly. "We went to town every once in a while, and had some acquaintances we tried to keep in touch with, but truthfully most of my social experiences involved watching really cheesy movies over and over again. Which makes me an expert on pop culture, but virtually ignorant on how to interact with people in the real world." My arms stretched and bent in odd angles, as I tried like hell to zip up the back of my dress without assistance. "It's odd though, because I don't think I ever realized how different humans were from protectors until today. They just have so much more freedom when it comes to living their lives. They can have whichever jobs they want, they don't have to worry about bondmates or being eaten by a vampire. It helps to live blissfully unaware of monsters, you know?" I frowned, thinking for a minute. "Though, to be honest, maybe a lot of that freedom is an illusion for most humans too."

"Ooh, I love that dress, you're so getting it." Izzy's voice rattled above my head and I looked up to find her peeking over the barrier between our dressing rooms. I twitched, pulling awkwardly against the spandex-like material. Catching the movement, she frowned. "Never mind, you don't look comfortable. Rule number one," she held up a single finger, "never buy something that doesn't make you feel awesome. Next option." She ducked down, disappearing back into her own room.

I could get behind that kind of logic. "Forget growing up away from protectors, what was it like growing up *with* them? And with Theo? And what's Reza's deal? Her personality is straight out of Mean Girls. She even kind of looks like Regina George."

"I love that movie!" Izzy swore softly as she zipped up her dress. "Too tight, this won't work."

I pulled on a burgundy dress that was flattering without being too revealing for my comfort. "I like this one."

Izzy's head reappeared over the partition, the top of her body housed in a bright blue monstrosity that belonged on either an unlucky bridesmaid or in an eighties movie.

"Ew, veto," I blurted out, but then immediately covered my mouth. Maybe I wasn't supposed to be honest about these things? Or at least not *that* honest. "I mean, unless, you know, you really like it. Because some people must, right? Since when you think about it, someone had to design it and decide it was good enough to sell in a store. It's not quite my taste, but I don't really have any sense of fashion in the first place, and plus it kind of reminds me of something you'd find in a Molly Ringwald movie, and I've always really liked her."

She laughed, the grin on her face so big that it went all the way up to her eyes. She laughed with her whole face. It was contagious. "I tried this one on for shits and giggles. Rule number two—it's never good to take yourself too seriously." She scrunched her nose and winked, making her look even more pixie-like than she already did. "But, as for your questions, growing up with protectors was just—I don't know, normal? It's all I've known. And well, Theo's just Theo. He's not a horrible person. Or brother. He's just really hard on himself. He wants to be the best. My family defines our worth based on how well we excel in fighting. Actually, that's how most protector families are. Which makes sense, when you think about it. Our survival depends on our ability to kick ass. Getting beat by the new girl? Not exactly his finest moment." She paused a beat, blinking slowly as another huge grin spread across her face. "But definitely one of my favorites."

Izzy's head disappeared and I heard her fall and trip next door, followed by a barrage of colorfully creative swear words.

"This dress requires more coordination than sparring," she mumbled, her voice mottled by fabric. I heard the sound of a zipper, and then the soft crackle of tulle as she tossed it aside. "And as for Reza. Well, she's just used to being the best. Her mother's the Headmistress of the Academy and really hard on her. That kind of pressure can turn people a bit sour, you know?"

"Oh, I didn't realize. That must be stressful."

"Don't go soft on me, Max. Parental expectations are no excuse to be a bitch. Theo's been in love with her since we were kids though, so I've had to listen to him singing her praises for years. I don't know, maybe I'm just bitter. I think part of him wanted to beat you today to show off for her. Kicking ass is kind of like protector peacocking."

"Peacocking?" I opened the dressing room carrying two dresses that I didn't hate. Not bad for my first actual shopping experience. Not quite on par with a Pretty Woman shopping spree, but I was pleased with my choices.

"Peacocking—you know—guys trying to impress girls they're interested in by demonstrating their primal value and physical prowess." She furrowed her brows, her voice deepening into a mocking lull. She paused a beat, thoughtful. "It's like caveman science. You know, I'm tempted to get this awful dress to wear when I need cheering up. It's so wonderfully ridiculous, don't you think?"

I looked at her thoughtfully, assessing. This must be what it was like to have a girlfriend.

Fun.

"Izzy, can I ask you something?"

"You just did," she winked. "Sorry, I hate when people say

that, but yeah, shoot." She walked over to a large wall of shoes, pulling a few out to match with our dresses.

"Do you know why everyone stares at Cyrus? It's like all eyes go to him the second he's in the room. Like he's a movie star or something. It's a bit weird, don't you think?"

Her hands paused on a pair of high black stilettos. "You're kidding right?" When I shook my head, she continued. "Well, he's one of the only protectors to take on a vampire solo and live to talk about it. There's a reason we hunt in teams. And Cyrus, well, he took on two. At once. Story goes that he saved Headmistress Alleva from a particularly gruesome duo, walking away from the battle with only a few superficial injuries, excluding some permanent damage to his leg. After that, he sort of disappeared from the protector world until you guys showed up last night. And I mean, he was gone for almost two decades, so it wasn't like he took a sabbatical or anything. For a lot of people, when you guys walked in yesterday, it was like seeing a ghost. A really famous one."

"Like Casper? Only less friendly." I covered my shock with a soft smile. That explained his occasional limp and extreme distaste for vampires. Not that any protectors were fans of the creatures from hell. But I wondered why in all our years, he'd never told us that story. Come to think of it, I didn't know much of anything about Cyrus before he took us in. His life kind of became training us.

"By the way, remind me to grab you one of my extra thigh holsters. They're perfect for stashing your blades when you're wearing a dress and heels. Not that I'm expecting an attack tonight or anything, but it's always best to be prepared." Izzy walked over to the cash register, a heaping pile of cloth and dangerous-looking shoes in her wake.

"I knew that wasn't just a boy scouts thing," I muttered, hurrying to pick up the pieces of her abandoned trail.

"How are you girls doing? Having a good day?" An elderly

woman with long grey hair started inspecting our garments before nodding approvingly and ringing them up.

"I'm doing okay," I started, encouraged by the woman's soft smile to elaborate. "It was my first day at a new school today, so I was a little nervous about that. But also kind of excited. And also, this was my first time shopping with another girl, so that was more fun than I thought it would be. I've been feeling a little off though, so that might be the nerves. Or, you know, because it's that time of the month." I whispered the last part, before dropping my voice off altogether. The woman was staring at me like I was a hydra and Izzy was laughing behind her hand. "Er, what?"

Izzy laughed louder, before calming enough to answer me. "It's just, usually when people ask how you are, they don't really want to know and they don't expect an answer other than 'good' or 'fine.' You weren't kidding when you said you didn't have a huge social life back home were you?" My cheeks reddened before she continued. "Don't be embarrassed. I find your particular version of word vomit endearing. You're honest. It's refreshing." She leaned towards me, whispering quietly so the woman couldn't hear, "and truthfully, I think it's kind of strange that people ask questions they don't really want the answer to. Disingenuous."

"Oh," I said, still kind of embarrassed, but happy to have her in my corner.

Izzy laughed, turned to the woman, and announced loudly, "I, too, have my period at the moment. In case you were wondering."

The woman smiled tightly, took our credit cards, and bagged our outfits without another word. Laughing, we collected our bags and wound our way back through racks of clothes until we caught up with Eli and the girl clearly under his spell.

He looked up at our approach, a surprisingly warm smile on his face, like he was actually excited to see us back. "Ah, sorry Eilene, it looks like my friends here are through." He handed her a small piece of paper and winked. "Give me a call later, if you want. I'd love to show you a good time." His tone dipped low and seductive, making it abundantly clear what kind of time he'd show her.

I wasn't sure whose face was more red—mine or Eilene's.

TWO HOURS LATER, I EMERGED FROM IZZY'S BEDROOM, dressed in the burgundy dress, with a thigh holster and a pair of black heels that required far more focus to walk in than I needed when running through the forest at night. Her room was slightly smaller than mine, but it was filled with so many personal touches and such interesting decor that I practically wanted to move in myself.

"You look perfect, Max." Izzy was putting the finishing touches on her makeup, while I stared in awe at her sure strokes and precision. She looked at me out of the corner of her eye and smiled. "Do you want me to do yours too?"

"Yes, I mean, if you wouldn't mind, that'd be really great." I didn't add that if I were left to do my own makeup, I'd likely walk out of here looking like Pennywise.

She nodded, patted the seat next to hers, and proceeded to paint my face, sure to explain each step. I took mental notes, as if I were in a classroom, so that I could reproduce the results next time we went out. Cyrus was good at many things. Teaching me about fashion and makeup? Not one of them. And while I liked to think of myself as more of a Lara Croft than a Holly Golightly, it was nice to be able to embrace that side of myself every once in a while.

After a few minutes, Izzy pulled back, a huge grin on her face. "There. You look perfect, Max. Let's go find Ro and head out before Cyrus goes parental, catches a glimpse of how hot you look, and tries to keep you locked up here forever."

I blinked back at her, confused.

"It's a dad thing." I opened my mouth to argue, but she cut me off before I could say anything. "Yes, I know he's not your dad in the traditional sense, but trust me when I say he'd go parental if he saw you trying to leave right now. Eighteen years old or not, biological father or not, it doesn't matter. It's just how dads are. And whether he acts like a conventional father or not, Cyrus is probably more protective than the best of them."

I smiled back, pleased. Cyrus was kind of like my dad, in a weird Yoda-esque way. At least the closest thing I'd ever have anyway. Still, it warmed me to think of him 'going all parental,' whatever that meant.

That warmness dissipated almost immediately when the bathroom door connecting to another room burst open.

"You guys are going to Theo's party too then." Reza walked in before pulling weird pouty faces in the mirror, as she studied her dress. Her sequined dress was more like a gown, shimmering with a brilliant shade of emerald that reminded me of Declan's eyes. As she glanced discreetly at me, I noticed her blue eyes popped even more than usual, with dark rings of black and grey outlining them.

"Well, he is my brother," Izzy said, catching my eye in the mirror.

"Reza's your roommate?" I looked over at Izzy's sad acknowledgement, her mouth tightening a bit, before offering a small, commiserative smile. I'd never been happier to be rooming with Ro. I *so* needed to thank Seamus and Cyrus next time I saw them.

"It's really charitable of you, Izzy, to befriend the new girl. Now you'll both have a friend." Reza swiped on a dark shade of lipstick with a kind of precision that filled me with envy.

"Thanks, Regina. Are you planning on being this big of a jerk to my brother tonight, too? It is his birthday, and while he can be a total dolt sometimes, it would be nice if you actually treated him like a person for once." Izzy shoved her makeup back into the cabinet, not even sparing Reza a glance.

I swallowed my laughter, but couldn't keep the amusement from flashing in my eyes.

"I know that I'm powerful, but did I hit your head during training today? It's Reza. And no, I wasn't planning on being anything to your brother tonight. Atlas will be there, so I'll be occupied."

My stomach lurched at the idea of Reza's paws on Atlas. I paused, analyzing the unusual and unwelcome burning sensation that seemed to gather behind my ribs. I took a deep breath, dissipating it.

On second thought, they'd be perfect together. Neither of them seemed particularly kind. Their children would probably pop out wearing matching family glares.

8

MAX

Izzy, Ro, and I pulled up to a small club in a town less than a fifteen-minute drive from The Guild. Though the area wasn't highly populated, the club looked like something you'd find in a more metropolitan city. I wrapped my arms around myself, trying to hold in the excitement. One day in and I had already made an awesome new friend and was going out for my first evening...well, out. It was wild to think that two days ago, I was bundled up in a blanket at the cabin, watching Fresh Prince reruns.

Eyeing me, Izzy smiled. "It's pretty impressive right? Considering we're practically in the middle of nowhere, I mean. This whole block is actually owned by protectors, which means we can get in even though we aren't twenty-one. As far as protectors are concerned, if we're old enough to put our lives on the line saving humans, we're old enough to enjoy a drink or two—which is allowed here and on campus, as long as we don't go wild with the privilege." She swept her arms in front of her in an exaggerated gesture, like she was a tour guide. "They built the mall, restaurants, and the club here so that Guild members could have somewhere fun to go without driving to an actual city. I think it's partially to incentivize us to stick around and not go off searching for adventure once we graduate." She narrowed her eyes slightly, considering. "Plus I imagine that they prefer us not to spend time around too many humans. The chances of secrets getting out increase when there are more forbidden ears around to hear them."

Ro smiled when we walked through the front doors. "This is great. We didn't have anything like this back home." His voice wavered with excitement, and I smiled at the sound of it. Having him here with me just made the whole experience even better.

The club was huge, much larger than it looked from outside. Like The Guild, it seemed to be a unique mixture of old and new —the bar and walls looked like they were made out of refurbished wood, and industrial pipes and metals lined the ceiling and walls. And it was packed. If I had to guess, almost everyone from The Guild in our age bracket was here, as well as a healthy mix of what I was guessing were local humans. The stench of alcohol was mixed with artificial fruits and sweat, which should have been disgusting, but it kind of added to the atmosphere in an interesting way.

I'd seen Cyrus drink before, but I'd never been inside of a bar or around so many intoxicated people. A few girls were cackling in the corner, their peals of laughter forcing happy tears from their eyes. People swayed close to each other, bodies looping together in seductive movements. While I'd seen clubs and bars on television, I didn't expect them to be accurate portrayals. But they were. Even down to the couple fighting across the room and a lone guy slamming back shots by himself at the bar.

"Here, there's some people I want you guys to meet that actually don't suck." Izzy's hand grabbed mine, interrupting my perusal, and I latched onto Ro as she dragged us towards the bar so that we formed an awkward conga line. We stopped in front of a small group that was amiably talking and drinking what looked like beer. "Max, Ro, this is Jer, Mavis, and Sharla," she pointed to each in turn, "and I think you've both already met Arnell?"

I reached my arm forward, taking each person's hand in my own. I tried not to laugh at the way Ro maneuvered his body so that he was standing next to Arnell. Nor did I miss the way that Mavis studied Ro, with a calculated amusement. Maybe even a bit of a challenge.

"Izzy tells me you kicked Theo's ass today in training, is that true?" Sharla was tall, with curly brown hair, bright blue eyes, and deep, flawless skin. Like most protectors, she was lean with muscle, but there was a softness about her that made her seem more approachable than some of the other girls I'd seen around the campus. When I nodded in response she patted me on my back, a giant approving grin on her features. "Attagirl. He could use someone to take him down a peg. If I'm being honest, that's the best birthday present anyone could ever give him."

"I didn't see any of you in training today, are you guys still in school?" I asked. They looked about my age, maybe a couple of years older.

The one called Jer shook his head. He had dark red hair, so dark it was almost black, and warm honey-colored eyes. "No, the four of us make up a team. We're hoping that when Izzy graduates, she can join us." He leaned closer, his voice dropping down a few octaves as his eyes met mine. "And maybe you too?"

I cleared my throat, uncomfortable. "Er, how many people are usually on Guild teams?"

Frowning, Arnell walked over, draping his hand across my shoulder. "Usually anywhere between four and seven. It depends on the team's weaknesses and needs. They usually try to pair people with complementary skills and personality sets, while also making sure the individuals bond well together. Truthfully, I think that's the hardest formula to gauge, but usually the most important. Trust is key in our line of work. When it comes down to it, your team will either save you or get you killed."

Izzy looked over at me and winked. "You know, kind of like the Justice League, or the Avengers."

"Oh god, now there's two of them." Ro shook his head while Arnell ordered us a few waters from the bar.

I exhaled in relief. I knew that we were allowed to drink alcohol here, but my social skills were awful when I was operating at one hundred percent—who knew what I'd be like while intoxicated. I stole a sip of Cy's whiskey once while he was sleeping and I was definitely not a fan.

Mavis wandered up to a shorter guy around the bar and the two started dancing, moving closer and closer as they swayed to the beat.

"Do you maybe want to dance with me, Max?" Jer's voice was deep and soft, and the look in his eyes was friendly enough, if not a bit intense. He was unlike most boys I knew. Then again, I could count the boys I knew on one hand. Where Michael was gentle and shy, Jer was all sharp edges and mystery.

But Michael didn't work out so, maybe it made sense to give Jer a chance. "Sur—"

"Sorry, Jer. I've got first dance. And possibly the second and third, if I'm lucky." I turned around, startled, only to find my face pressed into a warm, hard chest. I looked up and found a familiar pair of clear blue eyes staring hard at Jer. As they moved down to catch my stare, they instantly warmed. "She owes me for kicking my ass today."

"Wade." I exhaled softly, trying to dispel the nerves that had suddenly taken up residence in my stomach. I really needed to ask Seamus what they put in the food.

Wade was dressed in a dark blue button up that brought out the color of his eyes and I suddenly found myself hyper aware of his proximity to me. Which was close. Like, very *very* close. "So, what do you say, Max? Care to dance?" The corner of his mouth lifted up in a soft smirk while I stared back awkwardly.

I swallowed, studying the crowd of writhing bodies around us. This was something I'd definitely never done before. And they certainly weren't doing the waltz. This was something that was more at home on the set of Dirty Dancing. Strange how you could put a sword in my hand and I'd happily hop around swaying to an invisible count in my head, but when you threw in fast music, tight dresses, and mood lighting, I suddenly felt like the clumsiest girl in the world. Not to mention that the few times Ro had caught me dancing around outside, he compared me to a frightened chicken. That didn't exactly scream sexy.

"Um," I started, "I think I might not be so good at this. I just want you to know that now, so if you'd, like, want to find a better partner, I'd totally understand."

"Not possible." He grabbed my hand and smiled. "Just pretend we're sparring," he paused, before leaning down and whispering, "really, really close together." I could smell the subtle linger of whiskey on his breath and found myself suddenly wanting some liquid courage of my own.

I cleared my throat, and nodded up at him, unable to formulate words for once in my life. Maybe this whole nervous thing could actually work in my favor for once.

"Just don't take the sparring analogy too literally. I don't want you to punch me or anything," he added before turning me towards him and dropping both of his hands to my waist.

My body erupted into flames, chills rushing towards every extremity as I recalled the last time we were this close: Wade on top of me, pinning me to the ground, his body caked lightly in sweat. I took long, steadying breaths in, trying to focus on the music and very unromantic things. Like pudding. And puppies. And vampires.

He swayed slightly, his hips grinding into mine. I followed the thrum from the music that was competing with the pounding beat of my heart. I looked up and found his blue eyes staring down at me unflinchingly. It was like he was studying me again, and I blushed under the scrutiny. What did he see that seemed to fill his gaze with confusion and something else I couldn't quite put my finger on?

We danced for three songs, none of which I'd heard before. Cyrus had a thing for the Rat Pack, and whoever we were listening to was no Sammy Davis Jr. My body followed Wade's movements effortlessly. He was a good partner. If left to my own devices, I'd likely wind up looking like a female Napoleon Dynamite. Which is to say, awesome. But also probably not the best for partner dancing.

"Look, I know it's not really my place. I know you just met me and I can't expect you to trust me yet, but—" he looked down, a crease appearing between his dark brows, "I just want you to be careful around the guys in The Guild."

"The guys? Why? Do you mean you?" I pulled my hands away from his arms, suddenly confused.

He chuckled and ran a frustrated hand over his face. "No, not me. And not all of the guys. Mostly just be careful around Jer. At least for now, until you settle in here."

"What's wrong with Jer?" Wade's eyes creased further at my question and I found myself enjoying the look of him getting flustered. For once, I wasn't the one who didn't know how to say things the right way. Looking at Wade's brightening blush and the way he started to speak only to stop several times, I decided Ro was right—bumbling goofs were quite endearing.

"It's just, well. He's a bit of a player. He has a reputation of going through girls like toilet paper—" he paused a beat, "well, maybe toilet paper is a weird analogy. But I just mean that I don't want you to get hurt. And I know you haven't been around a lot of people, I just wanted to make sure that you were aware. I don't really think that Jer is the guy for you. Does that make sense? I don't want anyone to take advantage of you or push you into something you aren't ready for."

I nodded, smiling at his ruffled words. "I appreciate the warning, Wade. Really, I do. But if I didn't make it abundantly clear during class today, I think I'm perfectly capable of taking care of myself, don't you? Sure, I'm a little new to social situations, and I might be a tad more naive than most of the people here, but I'm not completely dense."

He laughed, a deep but soft chuckle that had my chest pounding louder than the music. "Fair enough, Max."

We danced along to another song in silence, before he looked back down at me, a small drip of sweat carving down his chest. It should have grossed me out, but mostly it just captured my absolute attention as it disappeared behind his shirt.

"I'm glad you're here, Max Bentley. The Protector Guild is sure to be much more interesting with you around." His words slurred softly, and I was struck by the idea that he might actually be drunk. Which fit, because when I'd met him earlier, Wade didn't seem quite as forward as Eli and some of the other guys on the grounds. His fingers dug softly into my waist, thumbs dancing in soft circles along the silky fabric of my dress.

My blood started to tingle slightly with the feeling and I found myself struggling to focus on his words. What was it about the guys around here that had my hormones having a full-on fit? Maybe it was Cyrus's fault for keeping us cooped up too much. My hormones were starved. When I looked up, his entrancing eyes were on my mouth, his face significantly closer to mine. My stomach dipped low and I bent my head back, ready for his lips to meet mine. The energy around us practically buzzed with heat.

Until I remembered that this would be my second kiss this week or, well, ever, and that the first one was ruined by fish, and the second would be ruined by alcohol and a man who may or may not remember it in the morning. Decidedly, if slightly hating myself for it, I ducked at the last second. His mouth bumped softly against the side of my head, and I felt a moment of regret. The thought of kissing Wade was far more appealing than it should've been, considering I didn't really know him at all and I'd been planning my future with Michael just a few days ago. I needed to take a break on the boy front, diving in was not wise. And I'd seen enough TV to know that juggling too many crushes was a recipe for disaster.

"Sorry," Wade muttered, a fierce blush coloring his tanned

skin. He covered his eyes with his hands, rubbing furiously like he could make the moment disappear if he tried hard enough. "Shit, I shouldn't have—I'm sorry, can we just—would it be okay if we just forget that happened?" He peeled his hand away, looking at me sheepishly. "Please?"

I nodded, smiling back, somehow both happy and sad that I'd stopped him in time.

"Seriously, Max, I'm so sorry. Here I am warning you about guys who move too fast with girls and then—" he shook his head, his jaw muscles clenching with tension as he avoided my eyes. "I don't usually drink too much and after getting chastised by my brother in front of everyone, I went a little harder than usual before showing up here."

"Consider it forgotten, Wade, really." I paused, processing his overzealous words. "Wait. Your brother?"

"Atlas." His hand swept the back of his neck as he nodded. "I don't know if you remember him, but he was the grumpy guy running the sparring session earlier."

Did Wade think it was possible for anyone to forget who Atlas was? The dude's commanding presence was enough to make even Cyrus take notice.

I took in Wade's deeper skin and light eyes, unable to trace many similarities between the two. And as for their personalities? They couldn't be more different if they tried. "Atlas is your brother? Seriously? How did that happen? You're so friendly. Sweet even. And he's, well, not."

He chuckled softly, embarrassment still lightly coloring his features. The look on his face was so handsome and open that I momentarily regretted not letting him kiss me properly. "Yeah, he's a complicated person, but not usually as bad as he seemed today. He's had an especially rough few months." His hand squeezed the side of my arm and he turned back towards me, squaring his shoulders. Blue eyes glazed over slightly, and there was pain there—and frustration—that I hadn't seen before. "And to be completely honest, I'm not all that sweet. I'm going to go get some water, maybe some fresh air, and head back home before I say or do anything else I'll regret tomorrow. We'll talk in training, okay?"

I nodded. "Yeah, I need a break from dancing anyway. Do you know where the bathrooms are?"

He pointed to the back hallway, said goodnight, and started to walk away. After two steps, he turned around and grabbed my hand. "In case I don't have the courage to do this tomorrow." He kissed my cheek, his lips somehow both soft and firm, and my stomach lurched at the warmth left lingering on my skin. That small touch somehow had my body tingling in ways that Michael's kiss didn't. "Goodnight, Max Bentley."

With a soft smile, he left me on the dance floor, my stomach twisted in complicated knots.

Knots that only got more tight and twisty when my eyes met Atlas's across the floor. He was holding a beer which he drained in a single sip, his jaw muscles tensing. The signature glare I was becoming familiar with had me frozen in place. I dropped my eyes, no longer able to meet his stare and found Reza's arms wrapped around his right bicep. She was fawning all over him like she was an added appendage, and while he didn't seem to notice or mind that every atom in her body was glued to him, I couldn't help the small bubble of frustration brewing in my gut.

He followed my gaze and smirked when he noticed my leveled glare at Reza. Disentangling himself from her limbs, he grabbed her hand, turned his back on me and walked to the bar to presumably grab another beer. Sheesh, these brothers were going to drain the bar of booze by the end of the night. And clearly alcohol impaired Atlas's judgment if it made him fine with allowing Reza to linger in his company like a fangirl.

Swallowing hard, I shook my head in frustration. They were both free to do what they wanted. But some part of me couldn't reconcile the fact that someone related to Wade could want someone like Reza.

Then again, Theo was Izzy's brother, so what the hell did I know?

"That was pretty hot, Max. Wade isn't usually so forward."

Speak of the devil and she will come. I smiled up at Izzy.

"Everyone is forward and every girl is desirable when you have a little liquid courage, Izzy." I gave her a small grin before nodding to the back of the bar. "I'm going to run to the bathroom. I'll meet you and the rest of the group in a little while, okay?"

She nodded as my eyes found Ro in a back corner talking to Arnell. They were huddled close together, warm smiles across both of their faces. It was adorable and I silently hoped that whatever was brewing between them would continue. I obviously didn't know Arnell well but, like Izzy, there was something about him that was just innately loveable.

"And keep an eye on Ro, will you? I don't want to be an auntie just yet. Especially not before I've had a chance to level Arnell with my intimidating you-hurt-my-brother-I-hurt-you speech." I laughed before making my way through thrashing bodies to the back hallway.

There were several doors lining the wall, so I latched onto the handle of the first door on my right. It wasn't locked, so I walked in, the heavy weight of the door closing behind me, and felt along the wall until I found the light switch.

And then I wished with every fiber of my being that I'd left the room to the dark and kept scavenging along the hall until I found the actual bathroom.

Because this sure as hell wasn't it.

Soft moaning made its way to my ears and I blinked rapidly when I found my gaze leveled on a man's back, his pants dipped precariously low on his ass while he thrust into a petite redhead, her face smeared with matching red lipstick and a satisfied glow. It was the salesgirl from the boutique.

To my absolute mortification, I couldn't seem to look away. I'd seen sex scenes in movies, obviously, but it wasn't quite the same as the real thing. I wrinkled my nose briefly. I didn't think sex would be associated with a smell, but it was. There was a distinct scent encasing the room.

A laugh made its unwelcome way through my lips and I slapped a hand over my mouth when the redhead's blue eyes opened in embarrassment.

"Shit. I'm so, *so* sorry. I thought this was the bathroom, and clearly it's not and so I'm, you know, just going to go now. Good to see you again, though! You, you know, carry on. As you were. Happy orgasming and what not."

At the glower on her face, I immediately realized that my hand should have resumed its place over my mouth after the whole 'I'm sorry' part. Obviously, this wasn't a time to make new friends or start a conversation. Even I had enough social awareness to register that.

With a deep chuckle, the man turned his head and I was met with Eli's stare—his eyes dancing with mirth. "I thought that was you, beautiful. Care to join us?" Noticing my jaw drop, his smile grew and he winked. "Or, you know, you can wait maybe two minutes and then have me to yourself, if you prefer?" There was a hunger in his expression that had my heartbeat pounding. "Or, tell you what, I kick her out right now, and no waiting necessary. Your choice, really. If you'd like."

I turned around, finding my way back to the door, hearing only the sound of his bellowing laughter and a soft slap that made it abundantly clear the redhead wasn't overly enthused with his offer. She started bickering, but after what sounded like skin slapping on skin, her grunts of protest turned into a different sort of grunt.

Oh god, I needed to get out of here now. There were just some things you couldn't unhear or unsee. And this? This was definitely one of them.

"Leaving now this is me leaving, La La La, can't hear anything." I plugged one of my ears as my free hand tripped the switch back off. I clumsily made my way to the door, struggling to find the handle. In retrospect, I should have turned off the light after I found the door. I tucked that bit of advice away for later in case I was ever so unfortunate as to find myself in a situation like this again.

After a few agonizing moments that felt like years, my hands grasped onto the cool metal. Why didn't protectors have night vision? Evolutionarily speaking, that would've been really freaking helpful. I opened the door, Eli's mocking laughter still rattling around in my head.

I turned immediately, not ready to go back into the club after witnessing that interaction, my mind practically numb with the image of the woman's legs wrapped around Eli's waist. It was weird how I could easily take down a guy twice my size, but the second you put me in a situation like that, I was complete toast. Then again, I didn't think even growing up in a huge city, with a stellar social life, could have prepared me to handle Eli's knowing smile and laugh. And I hated myself for being partially intrigued by his taunts.

Making my way along the hall, I found the back exit. The club opened onto a narrow alley and I walked along the old brick walls, a soft yellow light from the main street brightening my way. The brisk night air did wonders to help me regain a grip on myself and I took several long breaths in and out, as the music from the club beat through the thick walls in a distorted rhythm. None of the guys back home ever had me feeling all twisty and gross like this. Then again, I didn't exactly have regular contact with the guys back home either. Maybe this was normal? If it was, Cyrus might have had the right idea, living in isolation on the side of a mountain. Much safer that way.

After five minutes, my heart stopped its erratic pounding and I found myself acutely aware that I still had to pee, never having actually made it to the bathroom. When I turned to walk back into the club, I was face to face with a lanky man in a stylish suit blocking my way to the door. His dark hair fell in soft curls down his neck, and while the alley was too dark to discern the exact shade of his eyes, I knew with certainty that their focus was on me.

"Um, hi. Sorry, I didn't realize anyone else was out here. I'm just heading back in now." I smiled nervously, waiting for him to step aside and open the door for me like a proper gentleman.

He lifted a perfectly shaped eyebrow and took a step closer instead, the scent of rich spices washing over me. "Stay a while, pretty girl. I can promise we'll have so much more fun out here."

"That's okay, I'm fine with having just normal amounts of fun on the inside of the building. You know, where there's other people. Besides just you and me." My voice trailed off and my eyes travelled around the vicinity, noting any potential weapons. Cyrus always told us we should be prepared to make the world our fighting ring, and after Wade's warning about the men at The Guild, I was a little on edge. "Not to mention that this whole alley thing is a little too Norman Bates for my taste," I whispered to myself, but the smirk on his shadowed face told me he'd heard me too. Probably not human, then. Taking down another protector would be more difficult, but definitely possible if my training session today proved anything.

He stalked closer, and I took in the dark stubble lining his perfectly chiseled jaw, the glimpse of his starkly white teeth peeking between his lips. It was strange how a man could look so beautiful and dangerous at the same time. Then again, living amongst a bunch of protectors, I would hopefully get used to that soon. I wondered, briefly, if he was part of The Guild or some other organization. The grounds were huge and I'd only met a couple handfuls of protectors today—it could take me months to familiarize myself with everyone.

Still, even if he was one of us, I didn't intend to stick around. I'd seen enough horror films to know that the girl who wandered off by herself into creepy dark spaces always died first. That was so not going to be me. Especially not on my first day living in the real world. I might not have a ton of worldly experience, but as I told Wade, I wasn't ignorant either.

Not wanting to stick around for another moment with his alarming stare, I stepped to the side and made my way around him. Just as my hand reached the crisp metal of the doorknob, a much-too-strong hand pulled me back against a chest that felt like it was made of granite. While I assessed my surroundings, I felt the soft brush of two elongated teeth along my neck.

Holy shit.

Okay, so this wasn't just a creepy serial killer, this was a full-on Dracula. I stopped breathing for an impossibly long moment, my brain going fuzzy with fear. I was going to die here. Alone. I mean, even Cyrus struggled with taking out vamps when he didn't have a full team backing him up.

Fine. I would die here, but I was not going to go down quietly. Ro deserved a better story of my death than that.

Pity party over, I steeled myself before bucking my head back. I dislodged the man's hold before his fangs could pierce skin. That's what he got for playing with his food instead of snapping my neck first. He wasn't easily shaken off, however, and before I could get away, he pulled me back by the crook of my elbow, throwing me against the wall. The force of the maneuver knocked the wind from my lungs and I could feel the coarse brick biting into the skin on my back. He was stronger than anyone I'd encountered. Much stronger. Cy's limp made a world of sense now.

The vampire's hand encased my neck, lightly squeezing my windpipe, while he assessed me. My hand slid discreetly down my leg, the vampire's eyes shining with curiosity as I slid my fingers between the seams of the high slip. Using sex appeal to distract a guy almost never failed in the movies. Who knew they were obtuse enough to fall for it in real life too?

I winked, disarming his attention briefly, while I wrapped my hand around the hilt of my knife and pulled it in front of me.

Without hesitation, I slashed the blade up, aiming for his chest. He moved at the last second, so fast that it was impossible to correct my attack. Instead of landing into his heart, the knife fell into his shoulder, up to the hilt. Before I had a chance to grab it back, he flung me to the ground, much harder than any protector could ever manage. As my right arm cracked against the concrete, I understood why it was such a big deal that Cyrus handled two of these guys on his own. They held far more power than we could ever dream of obtaining—no matter how much time we spent training.

I jumped up, keeping my right arm held tight against my chest, while I squared off. Ro and I practiced sparring with one arm, while injured, many times—Cyrus taught us to be prepared for everything. I kicked off my heels, vowing to never wear them again if I survived this. Using my speed and strength to advantage, I ran towards the wall before ricocheting off of it with my bare foot and climbing up the vamp's back in a move that mirrored one I'd used hundreds of times on Ro. The surprise attack left me enough time to retrieve my knife from his shoulder, but not enough to successfully land a hit in his chest.

As soon as my fingers closed around the hilt, I kicked off from his back, landing hard on the cement. A fresh slice cut my knee open as I tried to right my balance, but wound up in an awkward kneel.

His left fist came hauling straight towards my head, so I slid between his legs and kicked out his knees, barely concealing my smirk when he landed hard against the ground. I peeled my left arm back, which wasn't my most accurate of the two, and plunged the knife upward from the top of the vamp's stomach into his heart. The angle helped me avoid running into any of his ribs, but judging by the fact that his face contorted with anger instead of death, I must've hit just left of his heart. Crap. This was so much easier to do on a stationary practice dummy.

I backed away while he jumped up and closed the distance between us in a blink of an eye.

"Shit, you dudes are fast." I cursed and pulled my knife out of his chest, but not before he pinned me back against the wall, holding both of my arms with one of his hands. It was like my strength was nothing to him—I was a limp doll in his grip. I whimpered as the pain in my right forearm exploded all the way to my shoulder, sure that it wouldn't heal for at least a day or two. And even then, only if it was properly set first. And even then, only if I managed to survive this whole altercation. And that wasn't looking too likely at the moment.

I thrashed a few times, but couldn't get him to budge an inch. "What the hell is a vamp even fucking doing in protector territory anyway," I growled, frustration leaking out of me as I tried to scramble for my next idea.

The leech started quietly laughing, but hard enough that his body rocked against mine, each of his ribs clacking against me like the world's most macabre instrument.

I screamed as his fangs pierced my neck successfully this time, drawing a long pull of blood. He inhaled deeply and his body went into a frenzy, lapping up my blood. I kicked out, pushing against him as much as possible, but he was using his whole body to pin me down against the wall. If he were just a protector, I'd stand a chance, but Nosferatu here was stronger than five of me stacked together. Maybe even five of Ro.

Right when I was sure this was the end, that I was breathing my final breaths, the vamp was pulled from my body. The force, coupled with the awkward angle of his fangs' exit, gouged a large chunk out of my neck. Gross. The blood loss alone was enough to make me instantly dizzy.

When I looked over, expecting to see my rescuer—a thought that pissed me off, since I was no damsel—I found myself instead staring at the pony-sized dog that helped me out in the whole werewolf transgression. This big guy had a habit of showing up right when I needed him. I thought of myself as more of a cat person, but this Fido was slowly changing my mind.

His body held the vampire pinned beneath him, his teeth and claws ripping into the vamp's chest. I found myself momentarily sorry that such a fine suit would likely be in tatters. I shook my head softly to bring myself back to the fight—clearly this blood loss was messing with my brain. Welcoming the tag-teamed distraction, I grabbed my knife off the ground where it'd fallen.

The vampire threw Fido across the alley and I used that moment to slam my blade into the vamp's heart. Judging by the monster's sudden stillness, my aim was true this time.

The vamp's death confirmed, I allowed myself to slide down to the ground, leaning against the body as a makeshift pillow, while the dog walked up to me and started licking my wounded neck.

It was like I'd traded in one bloodsucker for another. I absentmindedly patted him on his head, hyper aware of the feel of his soft fur between my fingers. It was so much easier to focus on something pleasant than the amount of bright blood coating my body. My vision blurred in and out as I saw the club door swing open and several angry voices surrounded me.

And then, finally, everything went black.

9

ELI

"Yeah, baby, that's it," Everly or Eilene, whatever the fuck her name was, moaned in my ear.

It wasn't as seductive as she thought it was, but that probably had less to do with her and more to do with the fact that I couldn't get a certain someone out of my head. It'd been a day and still the only thing that I'd been able to think about since meeting Max Bentley was, well, Max Bentley.

Which, to be honest, wasn't the most unusual thing for me. I was very easily distracted by a pretty girl. And something about the weird mix of awkward, naive, and badass just put Max into her own category. So no, I wasn't entirely surprised that I was super attracted to her. I was, however, surprised to be thinking about her so obsessively while buried into Emily. And it wasn't like I could exactly get her out of my system either.

My dad had already given me an hour-long lecture before Max and her family even arrived about how I had to keep it in my pants where she was concerned. Maybe he was worried that I'd hook up with her, get sick of her, and then scare her and, by extension, Uncle Cyrus away. He'd been angling to get Cyrus back to The Guild for as long as I could remember. Hell, the man was my father's brother and I'd only met him maybe twice in my whole life. So I was under strict orders not to go scaring him or his adopted daughter off.

And of course, the fact that I couldn't have her, wouldn't have the chance to get her out of my system, just made her even more appealing. Which was so unbearably annoying.

So, until I could distract myself with someone else, the sales-girl from the mall would do as a nice secondary option. If I closed my eyes, it wasn't completely impossible for me to pretend like I was burying myself into someone else. Someone else digging fingernails into my back. Someone else tightening around my dick. Someone else—

"Yes, Eli, just like tha—"

I pumped harder, hoping the new rhythm would shut her up. The girl was pretty, and her voice was husky and filled with all the right moans, but she was ruining the fantasy my brain was conjuring up. And it was a great one, even by my standards.

The lights came on, but I kept going, not wanting to break the momentum just to start back up again. Whoever it was would hopefully just turn around and leave us at it. Or hell, they could even stick around and watch for all I cared.

A soft intake of breath and then a familiar quiet chuckle had my muscles clenching and my eyes suddenly delving into Ellen. Nope, still the same red hair, red lipstick, and red dress that I'd entered the club with. Damn, my fantasy was more realistic than I'd thought. I'd have fun with that later, when alone in my room.

"Shit. I'm so, *so* sorry. I thought this was the bathroom, and clearly it's not so I'm, you know, just going to go now. Good to see you again, though! You, you know, carry on. As you were. Happy orgasming and what not." The voice was coming from behind me and my muscles tensed at the now-definitely-familiar rambling. Even when she was bumbling and caught off guard, she was appealing. Was everything about her so damn endearing? It was infuriating.

With a laugh, I turned around to see her. "I thought that was you, beautiful. Care to join us?" I teased, relishing the surprise on her face, and the reddening shade of her cheeks. I could see embarrassment, but also a touch of intrigue as well. Her mouth opened, and I forced my eyes to move away from the parting of her tempting-as-fuck lips, only to get a glimpse of what she was wearing.

Her deep red dress wasn't nearly as revealing as the girl I was fucking, but that somehow made it hotter. Which was weird. It hugged her small frame, showing off the curves of her chest and hips just enough to tease, to make me want to rip it off altogether. Just one look at her, standing there, and I could feel myself growing harder inside Evelyn.

And the thought of Max watching me screw took me to a completely new level. I'd been half kidding about her joining in, but not anymore. Forget my dad's rules. "Or, you know, you can wait maybe two minutes and then have me to yourself, if you prefer?" Her dark eyes widened with shock as they met mine. I could tell she was trying like hell not to lower her gaze. "Or, tell you what, I kick her out right now, and no waiting necessary. Your choice, really. If you'd like."

And I meant it. It was her choice and if she'd take me up on the offer here and now, my promise to good ol' Seamus would be well and truly forgotten. I'd probably regret it in an hour, but at least she'd be out of my system and I could go back to my regularly scheduled programming.

She turned back towards the door, clearly at a loss for words, and started to search for the light switch and door. Guess my promise was staying a promise, at least for a little while longer, anyway. Dear old dad would be pleased about that.

"Seriously?"

I looked down, surprised to find the salesgirl still beneath me. I smiled sheepishly.

"You're being such a fucking pig, you as—"

I gave a few thrusts, shutting up her quickly, the pace sending her into a fit of groans.

"Leaving now this is me leaving, La La La, can't hear

anything," Max sang, her voice wobbly with embarrassment. She cast the room in shadow once again and I had to bite back another laugh as she tried finding the handle in the dark.

All too soon, she was gone. With the lights off, I turned back to the salesgirl, capturing her lips in mine. It was the first time I'd kissed her, and I caught her moan with excitement, imagining it coming from a different set of lips. The girl came, and the visual of Max thrashing around like this, tongue tasting mine with eager intensity, instantly pushed me over the cliff and I quickly followed her orgasm with my own.

Giving myself a second to gather my thoughts, I zipped up my pants and reached for the lights, shame filling me as I saw the adoration-filled eyes of the girl next to me—the girl who was most definitely not Max Bentley.

"You're a bit of an ass," she said, her snarky smile made macabre by her messy lipstick, and I unconsciously swiped at my own mouth in case there were any traces of it. "But still, that was pretty incredible, so maybe I'll call you again sometime for a pick-me-up."

With a quick peck to my cheek, she left the room. I was glad neither of us had any illusions about what this was. There was nothing more awkward than when a girl had the wrong idea and went and got too attached. Especially when I was always so clear to explain ahead of time that it was just sex.

I thought back to the blush coloring Max's face and groaned. My father would kill me if I'd embarrassed her too badly. Now that I wasn't currently balls-deep in someone, my head was less foggy. And I was fairly certain that I'd been way too forward with her.

Circling back into the club, I scanned the crowd, looking for a pair of dark eyes and long wavy hair. I saw her brother and Izzy, expecting to find her with them, but she wasn't. Catching sight of Atlas, I walked up to the bar, ignoring Reza who was draped like a curtain over his arm.

I rolled my eyes. Everyone knew that Alleva and Reza were

deep in the throes of plotting for a matchup with Atlas, but it still turned my blood cold to not see him fighting it more. He wasn't overly affectionate with her, and I knew he only entertained the possibility because he wanted to stay here with our team. And after Sarah, he was fairly certain he could draw the bond out for a couple of years. But Jesus did it suck to see him put in that position. Especially after everything he'd been through this year.

"Hey man," I said, grabbing a fresh beer. "Have you seen Cyrus's kid?"

Without a word, he nodded towards Rowan. He was on the dance floor with Arnell and most of the Ten team. As far as company, it wasn't the worst sort for him to get mixed with. Arnell was a pretty cool guy.

I shook my head, downing half of my beer in preparation for my apology. Liquid courage was a real thing and I was man enough to admit I needed it. "No, not him. Max."

Atlas's nostrils flared slightly, but he didn't say anything more. Interesting.

"I know she's here, but can't find her anywhere," I said.

He narrowed his eyes as he disentangled himself from Reza's grip, studying the people in the crowd. He moved away from the bar and I followed, confused by his precision and silence.

"Atlas, don't be ridiculous," Reza pouted, looping her fingers around his and tugging him back towards the bar. "Just have another drink. It's not our job to babysit the newbie."

Without bothering to respond, Atlas peeled each of her fingers off of him, one by one, breaking the link between them. Reza was left standing there with nothing but a pout and a brewing promise that he'd regret his choice—that, or Max would. If she really wanted to bond to him though, she'd need to learn one thing: Atlas never took a night off.

"Where did you last see her?" he asked, his voice more gravelly than usual. There was a warning there, and a frustration I wasn't accustomed to. Atlas wasn't exactly all fun and bubbles, but he usually wasn't quite this intense around me. The last few days he'd been especially unbearable and gruff. It was starting to make my homelife absolutely miserable.

Maybe I'd see if the salesgirl wanted to pay him a visit later. She seemed like she was generally down for a good time and Atlas could use a little...fun.

"Eli," he bit out, reminding me that I hadn't answered him. His jaw was pumping with impatience as he continued studying the room.

"Jeez dude, sorry, chill. I'm sure it's not that big of a deal. She just—er—encountered me while I was preoccupied with my date in one of the backrooms." I scratched the back of my neck, both of us scanning the crowd now. She didn't exactly know a lot of people yet, so it shouldn't have taken long to locate her. Then again, she was a lot shorter than most protectors, so it made the search process a bit more difficult. "I wanted to apologize. You know how Seamus is about Cyrus. Last thing any of us needs is for my dad to get on my back right now." Good old Uncle Cy might've been the more intimidating of the brothers, but my dad was no slouch.

Atlas looked at me, the tension in his face softening a bit as he processed my meaning. He nodded. "Maybe she's in the bathroom."

We walked towards the back, but after watching several girls enter and leave the girls' room, it became clear she wasn't there.

"She wouldn't leave solo, would she?" I muttered to myself, feeling guilty for making her uncomfortable. "I mean, would she even know how to get back by herself? Pretty sure she arrived with her brother and he's still here."

Atlas paused, running a hand through his hair. "Good point. She'd need a car." He blew out a slow breath as he leaned against the wall, watching lazily as a couple of girls walked by. I tried not to get annoyed that they were ogling him and not me. Not the time. "It's not like there's much trouble for her to get in around here. Maybe she just went for a walk or to take a call outside or something."

I scrunched up my nose, considering. "I guess."

"Wade was coming on a little strong too," he added, the words clipped. "So between him and you, maybe she wanted to call it a night and take the long way back. She's fast enough, could probably make the run in under an hour."

Tapping a finger on my lips, I took a few breaths, trying not to be insulted by his point. "Did you get a look at what she was wearing though?" I grinned at the memory. "Not exactly the sort of thing you take an evening jog in, you know?"

Atlas pushed the wall, not willing to engage with me anymore on this. "I need air, you should just head back in and try to salvage the rest of your night. Maybe see if you can distract Reza for a bit. I don't have the energy for her shit tonight."

"Yeah man, sure." I'd drunkenly hooked up with Reza once or twice last year and lived to regret it. She wasn't worth the drama. And I was especially uninterested in her tonight.

He took a step towards the back door and froze, every muscle in his body visibly tensed through his shirt.

"What's up? Change your mind about heading home? Want to just head across the street and play a game or two of pool?"

In a flash, he moved to the door and opened it, before stopping dead as soon as he crossed the frame. Curious, I followed him.

"Jesus," I said, my stomach churning with acid. "You don't think—she's not dead is she?" Max was draped against a guy, a giant dog guarding her with low, menacing growls. I moved towards her before running into Atlas's hand, which he'd pressed hard into my chest. "Is that—oh my god, is that a fucking hellhound?"

"And a vampire," Atlas added, his voice low and filled with steel. He was staring at the hellhound, their eyes locked in a weird battle of wills. "We won't hurt her, we're here to help. You have my word."

Was he seriously trying to have a conversation with a hellhound?

As if Atlas had uttered the magic words, the dog let out a little whine before nuzzling her hand. Sparing me a brief glance, Atlas moved slowly towards Max. There was blood—so much fucking blood—everywhere. What the hell was a vampire doing this close to our territory? They weren't ever that dense.

I watched her until I saw the almost imperceptible rise and fall of her chest. I breathed out in relief.

She was alive.

10

MAX

I ran through a lush forest, my bare feet sinking into the dirt. As I moved, the dark trees became mere shadows against the night. The vamp was on my heels, and though I couldn't see him, I could feel him—my skin tingling like a beacon. The scent of warm spices drifted through my nose.

Recognizing a familiar metallic glint, I stopped short, skidding along the dirt and brush. My knife dangled from a tree branch, the soft moonlight reflecting against the obsessively shined silver. Cyrus had gifted me that blade on my tenth birthday. I paused, jumping up to try and reach it. The pounding of footsteps behind me was getting closer, but I refused to look back, stretching my limbs as far as they'd go. But I still couldn't do more than ghost the tip of my fingernails against the handle.

I never thought a day would come when I'd wish for a pogo stick, but here it was.

Or maybe a ladder. That might be more practical. Or really, really high stilettos. Why was I barefoot?

"How were all three of you at Vanish last night and not one of you was aware there was a vampire hanging around outside? What the hell were you doing?"

That was strange, I didn't remember the vamp being a woman. Or having an Irish accent. He was dark and brooding, sure. His voice was *strong and sensual...but this, this was different. With a solid push off the ground I overextended my arm, my finger just barely brushing the tip of the knife. This was infuriating.*

"We were in a club. You know, loud? How were we supposed to know she was hanging around in the back alley by herself. What kind of girl does that? I mean isn't it part of the cultural zeitgeist that chicks are supposed to stick together in places like that? Besides, how the hell could we know that a vamp was going to attack so close to protector territory?" A pause, some throat clearing, "plus I was, er, occupied at the time."

He was gaining on me. Two breaths away. One. His long slender fingers reached out and grasped at my throat. I punched him in the gut and climbed up his body, which was almost a full foot taller than mine. If I couldn't get my hands on a pogo stick, a tall vampire would have to do. My hands clasped against the hilt of my knife. A moment went by until I paused. Why hadn't the vamp thrown me off or fought back? Instead, he'd let me use him like a rock wall.

And just as the strangeness of the moment sank in, I went sailing through the air, an awkward and flailing ball of limbs.

Okay, maybe he hadn't forgotten about me.

"Yeah, it's definitely unusual behavior for them. I've never seen one of the humanoids get that close to Headquarters. Wade, where were you?"

"I, uh, left a bit early. Had a bit too much to drink."

The thought of this vamp having too much to drink had my heart pumping hard in fear, guiding him to my arteries like a bat signal. He crawled over to me, moving along my body like a snake, until he held my hands above my head. I was struck by the realization that my right arm no longer hurt to the touch, and smiled. It was a strange thought to have moments before dying. But if I had the choice of dying with or without an injured arm, I'd happily take the latter.

Well, maybe not happily.

I tried to resist, thrashing around like a Magikarp, but to no avail. So this was going to be how I died? I'd always hoped it would be while doing something adventurous, like skydiving or zip lining. Or poking fun at Cyrus until he lost all control. This felt so...boring. An anticlimactic end to a frustratingly anticlimactic life.

Sharp teeth pierced my skin like I was nothing more than an apple, but it didn't hurt. Still, I screamed. Because vampire.

"Uh, why is she screaming? Jesus, go get Cyrus Dec, or my dad—and hurry. He already wants to wring our necks. She's here one day and almost gets killed."

"It's a dream, you bumbling shithead."

A black pony sailed through the air, dragging the vampire off me. The animal circled back and nudged me with its large head, prodding me with its hooves before calloused hands started to shake my shoulders— somehow both rough and gentle.

"Ponies don't have hands," I mumbled, my eyes cracking open briefly, until a painfully well-lit room had me snapping my lids closed again. "Oh god, death is fucking terrible."

I inched my head to the left while pushing myself up, trying to get a better feel for my surroundings, and moaned. The pain in my neck and arm weren't gone then I guess. If anything, I felt worse than I thought possible. No fight with Rowan or Cyrus had ever left me feeling like this. My blood felt like sandpaper rushing under my skin.

A soft chuckle brought my focus to a pair of light brown eyes.

"Welcome back to the land of the living, beautiful." Eli smiled down at me, his large hand cannibalizing my own. "It figures you'd try and take on Cyrus's reputation after spending only one day in our world." His tone was joking, but worry and fear were mapped across his face. And maybe a little guilt?

"Wha—" I cleared my throat, my mouth dry and bitter. "What happened? Where am I?"

"How the hell is she already awake? Eli, go get Cyrus and Seamus. Tell them she's up." Atlas barked the command, not sparing me a glance while he paced back and forth in the room.

I turned my head, carefully, taking in the new surroundings. The room was cold, white, sterile, and bright—so fucking bright.

The light was practically drilling a hole through my retinas. I inhaled deeply, scrunching my nose at the stark scent of antiseptic. My body was sore. It didn't help that I was lying on a narrow bed that was more rock slab than mattress.

"This is your hospital? I feel like I'm in a morgue," I mumbled, my voice dry and cracked. If I weren't so disoriented, I'd be momentarily pleased by the new croony tenor.

Wade walked up, grabbing the hand left vacant by Eli's departure. "Glad to see your sense of humor is still intact." His pale eyes dropped down slightly, and he cleared his throat awkwardly. "I'm sorry I left you like that last night. Maybe if I'd stayed, or not had so much to drink, this wouldn't have happened."

I squeezed his deceptively soft hand. What a weird thing to blame himself for. "It's not your fault. But, um," I cleared my throat to no effect, "while we're on the topic, what exactly did happen?"

"You don't remember?" Declan's brows creased in concern, and I was struck by how strikingly beautiful she was. Like a concerned fairy. They were all maddeningly beautiful. Even Atlas the Asshat.

"Atlas the Asshat, eh? I'll have to use that sometime." Wade's face crinkled with unshed laughter.

Shit, I must've said that out loud.

"You did. It's the effects of the medicine," Atlas said as he turned to Declan, ignoring me once more. "Also probably why her memory is a bit muddled about last night. She's likely also feeling disoriented." His words were cold, clipped. I felt like a boring lab rat that he was being forced to observe and take notes on.

"Is he always such an emotionless jerk?" I mumbled.

"Still speaking everything out loud, firecracker." Declan muffled her laughter as she studied her friend.

"Oh, that one I meant for him to hear." I paused briefly, looking up at them all. "Seriously though, can someone tell me what happened? Last thing I remember I was fighting off a vamp."

Like clockwork, all three of their faces darkened.

Atlas looked from Declan to Wade and blew out a huff of air when he realized he was the only one in the room who was there, besides me obviously. "I only caught the last second. You were leaning across a dead vamp, and almost as soon as Eli and I found you, you passed out. Likely from all of the blood loss. There was...a lot."

"Oh, did I say something snarky and hilarious?" I flourished my hand around and grunted, remembering all too late that my right arm was still a wreck. And last night? How long was it going to take for me to heal?

"What are you talking about?" A crease formed between Atlas's dark brows, and I dropped my eyes, unable to maintain contact with his. I noticed a scar on his arm, it was flat and only a shade or two removed from his skin tone, so it was difficult to see. He'd never been this close to me before, so it wasn't something that caught my notice. But it did now. Protectors rarely scarred. Noticing my appraisal, he shifted uncomfortably and pulled his sleeve down.

"You know, like Buffy. She always says something witty and awesome whenever she dusts a vamp," I mumbled, partially distracted by his closeness. Something about his presence just overwhelmed me completely. And now I was sitting here, surrounded by three of the most powerful people in The Guild. It was a lot for a girl to handle, especially after such an ordeal.

"You're a strange girl, Max Bentley." Wade shook his head and rested his hand on my hip. After a moment, he realized how close his grip was to my lady bits and he moved his hand sharply to my calf. I smiled at the flush in his face.

"So no witty remark for the dead vamp then?" I conceded, frowning slightly. Next time maybe. "Did you see the giant dog? Please tell me you saw the giant dog. And that she's alright. Second time now that she—or he—has saved my life."

"Giant dog? You really must have hit your head hard, Max." Wade's eyes shone with worry, but I caught the way Atlas looked around the room, scratching his stubble as soon as I made mention of the dog.

"The dog, unfortunately, is being kept in the lab here." Cyrus's voice boomed across the room and Declan and Wade parted, allowing Ro to grab the seat by my head. "Ro and I just came back from talking to the head of research. It's clear the hellhound means no harm, but protectors are stubborn and hellhounds have a bad reputation. So they won't listen to me and are going to keep him locked up for now. If the beast was smart he'd have run off, but he refused to leave the grounds once Atlas and Eli brought you back." There was venom in his words and I wondered, briefly, how long Cyrus would be able to put up with someone else pulling rank and disagreeing with him. That didn't fly in our little cabin-world.

"Holy shit, she wasn't lying about the giant dog then?" Wade asked, his eyes widening as he watched Cyrus approach.

"You're awake already," Cyrus mumbled, ignoring him. "That's good. Very good. Sometimes protectors don't wake from vampire bites. And they almost never heal."

My eyes fell to Ro, who hadn't said a word since walking into the room. His head was bent down, his hands digging into the hair on the back of his head. I lifted my left arm and ran my fingers through his, pulling his hands away before he gouged out a chunk of his scalp. When his face lifted to meet mine, it was pale, empty of his usual mirth.

"What, no winning commentary for us all, Ro?" I tried to lighten the mood, but at the wispy sound of my voice, the frown creasing his forehead only deepened. "Don't worry, brother dearest. I'm perfectly fine. Was told I handled that vamp like a pro. Full on Buffy-style retort and everything. You should've seen it—spectacular, I'm sure."

"You lie." The shadow of a grin danced across his face. "The first thing I asked Eli once you were stable was whether you said something ridiculous after sticking your knife in the parasite's heart. You were out cold."

I winked at him before turning my attention back to Cyrus. "What do you mean protectors sometimes don't wake from vampire bites?" I mean, I knew that was true with werewolves, so I guess it made sense. But damn, that was something they should be broadcasting during every spar session: 'may die if Edward gets toothy.' "And what do you mean the bites don't heal? I thought we were supposed to have super healing powers?"

Cyrus cleared his throat and looked about the room avoiding eye contact. It was unusual for him to be so flighty. "Like with werewolves, the venom vampires leak into their bite can be fatal for protectors. There is always lasting damage though." His eyes drifted solemnly down, leading my gaze to his leg.

"Your limp? That was caused by a vamp bite?" I asked, anxiety rasping my voice. So the story was true then. He'd taken on two vamps and lived to tell the story. Part of me was convinced it was just an old wives' tale.

"Aye, the teeth hit bone" he responded. "But you're already awake and speaking, and the wound doesn't seem too deep. If you're lucky you'll only be left with a scar and some minor discomfort around the area."

Great, one day as a student at The Guild and here I was eternally injured already. Just my luck. Ah well, at least I was alive. And, while I was certainly sore, my arm hurt far more than my neck did. I was afraid to take the bandage off though, not ready to deal with whatever brutal wound was underneath. The room was uncharacteristically silent while everyone looked everywhere but at me, until my eyes met a pair of dark ones.

Atlas. A brief flicker of something flittered behind his gaze, but it was gone almost as soon as I noticed it. And then, as if I'd imagined it, he looked elsewhere.

I cleared my throat, uncomfortable with the silence. "Also, what the hell is a hellhound?" I paused a beat. "Pun intended." Even though it wasn't.

"A hellhound is a very rare creature from the hell realm. One has not been seen in our world in at least a century. Probably quite a bit longer. We know almost nothing about them." Seamus was standing behind Cy. I hadn't even noticed him before. Whatever meds they had me on were seriously messing with my usually stealthy senses.

I turned to Cyrus and then to Ro. "This is the same Fido from back home? I thought so when it rescued me last night, but things happened so fast I couldn't really be sure. And I was more invested in killing the vamp than doing an identity check."

Ro nodded and resumed his internal sulking. His mouth opened and closed and I waited patiently for him to say what he needed to say. It was the only way with Ro. "I'm so sorry I wasn't out there with you, Max," he blurted, words in a hurried rush. "If that hound hadn't found you first, who knows what would've happened. I mean, fuck." He stood up and turned. Several uneven breaths wracked his body, until he suddenly struck, punching a hole in the wall.

That was Ro, though. Even when he was emotionally distraught, he had to show off how badass he was.

Peacocking. I think that's what Izzy called it.

Ro glared at me, but soon broke into a soft chuckle, dissolving the tension. I guess I still wasn't totally aware of what was coming out of my mouth, then.

Cyrus's words caught up to me and I snapped my focus in his direction, flinching slightly from the pain in my neck.

"Wait, so you're telling me this dog saved my life twice. And instead of giving it the world's largest Milkbone, the protectors here have him locked up in some creepy laboratory?" Uncharacteristic anger bloomed in my blood. I was getting that dog out if it was the last thing I did. I owed him.

Seamus's eyes traveled to the ground, unable to hold contact with mine. Good, he should feel bad. And the expression on Cyrus's face—his lips pulled into an impossibly tight line—told me that he wasn't too happy with his brother about the situation, even if it wasn't completely Seamus's fault.

Seamus cleared his throat before searching around the room, like he was trying to string together a reasonable explanation. "It's complicated, Max. Not only are hellhounds extremely rare, they are typically associated with powerful demons. They are dangerous and highly unpredictable. It's unusual for one to take an extended interest in anybody, let alone a protector. This is twice now that he's followed you and saved you from hell beasts. We can't just ignore that and send him off into the world. Until The Guild can be sure that he means no harm, they'd prefer to keep him locked up." I opened my mouth to argue but Seamus lifted his hand to silence me. A strategy he shared with Cyrus— and one I was *so* not a fan of. "We have, however, made sure that he won't come to any harm while he remains here. We just can't risk inciting panic when people see a potentially dangerous, potentially evil beast roaming around the grounds. No matter how good its intentions seem to us now. We have no way of knowing for sure."

I growled, frustration spilling from my every pore, before turning to Cyrus. "Well, take me to him then. I'd like to at least thank him for saving my neck, literally, twice now. And then I would like to apologize for getting him stuck in some creepy ass dungeon, while researchers treat him like some rare zoo exhibit."

Ro stood next to me, crossing his arms and facing off against the odd assortment of people in the room. Declan and Wade were so silent, I almost forgot they were here. I patted Ro's side, appreciating the show of solidarity. If no one would let the dog out, we'd find a way to break him out ourselves. Until then, we'd bide our time. I could be patient. Or at least I would try.

"Right now, Max, you need to rest. You've lost a lot of blood, and while you heal fast, you will need to stay down here for a while. Vampire bites are nasty business. You're in for a few rough nights." Cyrus laid a hand on my foot in an uncharacteristic show of affection.

"I'm staying down here with her tonight." Ro squared his shoulders, daring Seamus to challenge him.

"No."

My head spun and I cringed at the twinge in my neck. It wasn't Seamus who rejected him, but a small, hunched over old woman. Her hair was cropped short and spiky, sticking up everywhere as if she'd been electrocuted. I liked it.

"Who're you?" I asked, too shocked by her appearance to be polite. Protectors had advanced hearing, and not one of us heard her until she was almost right by my bed.

"Your nurse. And I say you need rest and peace. Two things you won't get if I allow you to keep this harem of misfits hanging around your bedside." Her voice was soft and wispy, even though the words were firm. With a smiling eye, she turned to Atlas. "That means you too, boy. No way am I letting you butter me up this time. You'll all leave and return tomorrow for visiting hours. Then, in a couple of days, Ms. Bentley here will likely be cleared to bed rest in her own room."

Ro opened his mouth to argue when Atlas dropped a hand on his shoulder. "Trust me, she's not someone you can win an argument against."

She peeled the dressing back from my neck as the corners of her mouth bent down in a small but kind frown. "I could've sworn there were deep incision marks when I dressed this earlier." She stepped back, her brows pointing towards each other as she studied me. Her eyes narrowed further as she moved from watching me to watching Cy. "You were here when I dressed the wound, no? Tell me I was seeing things, that there weren't clear-as-day bite marks?"

Cyrus walked over to the other side of my bed and lightly pulled my head towards him, examining my cut himself. Worry lines pebbled his forehead. "Impossible." Instead of meeting my eyes, he looked at his brother.

While they had their weird silent conversation, I resisted running a hand over my neck. "What's the big deal?" I asked. "As the one snacked on recently by a vamp, I can assure you that there is in fact a bite wound. Plus, my neck stings like a bitch, so I know there's an open wound."

"A wound," Seamus said, stepping closer to me so that he could inspect my neck for himself. "I imagine it's from where the fangs were pulled at an odd angle, gouging a chunk of your flesh out. That trauma is still healing, but it is now quite superficial, like a scrape, and will heal like all your wounds heal. The incision point, though—from the fangs? It's so faint that it's practically gone. I saw you when they brought you in. That bite was deep. It should take months, maybe even years to get healed to this level."

"Impossible," Cyrus said again. "I've never seen a protector heal like that from a bloodsucker bite." His calloused fingers pressed lightly against the untouched skin surrounding the injury. "And it's not even like she's a particularly fast healer, as far as our kind goes. Her arm is still a mess from the breaks."

I furrowed my brows at that last part—it sounded danger-ously close to an insult. "I don't heal *that* slowly," I mumbled.

"What does this mean?" Eli asked. His expression was odd, like he couldn't tell whether to be pleased or worried by the news. That made two of us.

"We don't know. But for now, no one in this room discusses Max's situation with anyone else," Cyrus said, his dark eyes glaring daggers at the weird band of protectors scattered around my bed.

"Agreed," Seamus said, nodding his head for emphasis. "We can't keep the attack quiet, but all anyone needs to know is that Max was injured. The official account will be that she wasn't bitten—especially since the bite will be gone by morning at this rate. We'll study the vampire's body." His warm eyes, the exact shade as Cy's, looked from me back to his brother. "Maybe there's a reason his venom was less intrusive."

I shuddered, feeling bad for whoever had morgue work tonight—and equally bad for whoever got stuck hauling the vamp's body back from the nightclub. I had a feeling that it was somebody in this room.

"Understood," Atlas responded, soliciting a humorous echo of nods from his team members. With a final nod in my direction, he gestured to Wade, Eli, and Declan before walking through the door—the latter three sending me brief, sad smiles before following suit. They were such an odd group, but I was glad to know that they got me back here safely.

Cyrus pressed a soft kiss to my forehead and turned without saying a word, leaving with Seamus.

Ro and I stared after him, our mouths gaping. He'd never done that before. Cy's version of parental affection was flinging darts at us while we tried to dodge them.

"Maybe he's the one who hit his head tonight?" I looked up at Ro as a mixture of confusion and warmth trickled through my body.

With a soft chuckle, Ro turned to the nurse and put on his best impression of Cyrus. "You better take good care of her. I'm not against beating up an old woman if I have to."

The nurse laughed, clearly able to spot the lie as quickly as I could. "Who are you calling an old lady, kid?"

She straightened her spine a bit and Ro sunk. "Sorry, no offense was meant."

"Night Ro." I pulled his sleeve slightly to get his attention back to me. "Be sure to break me out of this joint tomorrow or as soon as possible. This bed feels like a slab of concrete."

"Always so dramatic, Max." He rolled his eyes before exiting and I found my gaze suddenly monopolized by the most wrinkled face I'd ever seen.

"You sure you should still be working? Don't protectors have, like a retirement program of sorts?" I asked, scrunching my nose. I had no intention of working for them my whole life and someone her age should be out enjoying the world.

Belatedly, I muttered an apology. That was probably one of those things I was supposed to edit out before speaking. Cyrus was always so gruff, it sort of stung to realize I was adopting that trait and that it wasn't the norm. I needed to invest in a back-space button for my mouth.

She let out a deep laugh, not offended by my lack of filter. It was refreshing. "I'm a volunteer. When you're my age with no family, you get lonely. The Guild has been kind enough to let me offer my services here. The name's Greta, by the way. In case you were ever planning to ask."

I blushed, suddenly embarrassed by my lack of manners. "Right, sorry. Nice to meet you Greta. I'm Max."

"I know who you are Maxine Bentley. You and your family have unsettled the dust, storming through here out of nowhere like you did." I cringed at her use of my full name, earning me a chuckle. "Get some rest, I'm retiring for the evening but there's a button next to your bed if you need me for anything. I'm a light sleeper, so I'll respond almost immediately."

With a wink, she reached for the door handle and left, but not before a plastic card fell from her pocket to the floor.

11

MAX

I think I counted to thirty-seven before I couldn't handle waiting any longer. I jumped from the bed, momentarily dizzy from the pain in my arm. Too bad the break wasn't healing as quickly as the bite. My bare feet were freezing against the scuffed floor, as I bent down and picked up the rectangular piece of plastic. Though I'd never seen one before in real life, I watched enough spy movies to know that this was some sort of a key card. And my gut told me that it would open the way to my hellhound.

Maybe the old nurse wasn't so bad after all, almost like my very own protector-godmother.

Not wanting to wait another second, I opened the door, exhaling in relief that she'd left it unlocked for me. After a quick glance left and right down the hall, I was satisfied that I was alone. There were only three other rooms in this hall, and they all looked to be either empty or housed with sleeping patients.

Light on my feet, I all but ran down the hall, the exhilaration of acting out my Nikita fantasies suppressing the pain in my neck and arm. When I reached the end of the hall, I looked to the left. This new hall was filled with dozens more doors that looked more or less like the one I'd just escaped. Everything was a crisp white color, illuminated by the flickering lights running along the ceiling. Turning my head gingerly to the right, I almost screamed in triumph.

A metal door, complete with a superspy scanner. Practically skipping, I pulled the grey card out and muffled my shout of glee when the heavy metal door unlocked.

Expecting to find a collection of supernatural beasts, I looked around and deflated. This hall held nothing, just thick metal walls. It didn't help that it was practically black as night in here either, any light from the hall disappearing as the door closed. Still, I wasn't ready to give up on my quest, so I ran my hands along the wall until they guided me to the other end.

The hall stopped short after only a few feet and I momentarily started to panic. This wasn't a giant hall, this was a tiny metal coffin. For someone used to living in the great outdoors, I'd never experienced the absolute torment of confined space before. The heavy beating of my heart told me that I might have a touch of claustrophobia. Good to know. Living in a forest didn't provide too many opportunities for feeling trapped. Not in the conventional sense anyway.

Frantically running my hand along the opposite wall, I found a small plastic box protruding at about my shoulder level. Tracing my fingers along the edges, I breathed a sigh of relief when I reached a miniature lever and lifted. Soft digital lights pierced the heavy darkness and I found myself confronted with another scanner. Swiping my borrowed card, I smiled when the door clicked open. This must be some type of airlock or failsafe in case one of the creatures made it past one of the doors.

Closing the door quietly behind me, I looked around. This hallway was softly lit and looked much more high tech than the hospital wing I'd just come from. Careful to stay quiet, I crept along—just in case any of the lab geeks were still awake. I doubted they'd be okay with me making myself at home in their super-secret lair.

The lab looked to contain a wide variety of species, some

better protected than others. There were several rooms, for instance, that looked like a nuclear bomb couldn't break the inhabitant out—the walls and door made of a solid, unusual metal. None of these rooms had windows or scanners for me to swipe into, so I had no idea how I'd find my hellhound. Greta didn't exactly leave me a map.

The low murmur of approaching voices startled me into a girlish jump, and I slammed my fist against my mouth to prevent the escape of the matching squeal. Looking around the hall, I trembled with anxiety—getting caught now made the whole stealth thing null—I might as well have stayed in my uncomfortable bed, waiting for Greta to wake me in the morning.

At the last moment, I noticed a door unlike the others. This one appeared to be normal, with no extra protective measures, so I reached for the handle. The soft click of the door opening calmed my rapid heartbeat, and I threw myself behind it just as the soft voices turned the corner.

I backed slowly into the room, my lips pressed together in a silent prayer that they didn't see me. I knew that once I was caught down here, it would be practically impossible for me to orchestrate another trip. The voices grew closer, closer, closer, and then they started to fade away. Letting out a long breath, I backed against the cool wall, and glanced around the room.

Unlike the others, this room was filled with a series of glass walls that allowed the researchers to look in on the inhabitants. That meant my poor hellhound was locked up in a glorified zoo. Anger coursed through my veins. How long would they keep him here?

The rooms were all dark, making it impossible for me to discern whether or not they were vacant, except for the last wall on the left where a soft glow lit the area.

I made my way to it.

And then I let out a happy rush of air when I came face to face with a large dog, whose eyes were on the same level as mine. He was even more giant than I remembered. Intimidating, even.

This close, I could almost understand why the protectors were afraid of him. Especially if there wasn't a lot known about the species.

Cyrus sure as hell had never mentioned hellhounds. And the only version I'd ever heard of had three heads and was found in Disney's Hercules.

"It's you." I pressed my hand against the windowed wall and studied the beast that had saved my life not once but twice. I closed my eyes, trying not to focus on the fact that in the last few days, I was attacked by two hell realm creatures. It was a lot to process. Especially considering I'd never seen a supernatural creature outside of my books before last week.

The hellhound's coat was pure black and looked like velvet. There was a small patch of grey surrounding his right ear. It almost made him look dog-like, silly even—insofar as a giant hellhound the size of a horse could look silly. But still, kinder perhaps? His eyes were a dark amber and looked far too intelligent for a domestic animal in the human realm. There wasn't any animosity in those eyes, though there was an alertness, a hesitation.

I watched, in turn, as he studied me, with almost as much critical focus as I was studying him. He walked slowly towards the windowed wall and I felt my heartbeat pick up with the dregs of fear. I doubted he could break through the small prison if he wanted to, but still, the creature was far more intimidating than any animal I'd seen before—his predatory stare more startling than even a lion.

Not that I'd ever really seen a lion stare at me before.

When he licked the spot where my hand remained pressed and let out a friendly whine of recognition, I exhaled. He hopped down on his front paws, his butt in the air, and wagged his tail.

My shoulders loosened, recognizing the universal sign of a friendly pup who just wanted to play. It seemed suddenly ridiculous that protectors feared him.

"I'm sorry I got you locked up in here, boy." I paused, considering. "You are a boy aren't you?"

The friendly chirp of a bark confirmed that he was and also that he could understand me when I spoke.

I smiled and sank to the floor, suddenly overcome by exertion. I must've lost even more blood than I'd originally realized. I leaned my forehead against the cool glass and looked on at my strange protector.

"Why have you saved me twice?" I asked, fully aware that there would be no way for him to respond to such an open-ended question. He laid down next to the window, his fur pressed to the glass as if he wanted to be as close to me as he could. Warmth spread through my body, and it felt almost as if we were meant to find each other, that he was made to be kept close. I shook my head and laughed at the thought—as if a hellhound could be kept as a mere house pet.

Still, struck by an idea I made eye contact. "How about I ask you questions and if the answer is yes, you bark once. If no, do nothing."

He barked once in response and my face split in what likely looked to be a maniacal smile.

"Okay great." I paused a beat, searching for a good place to start. "When the werewolf attacked," I started, "had you been tracking it?"

No bark.

"Had you been tracking me, then?"

One bark, soft and friendly.

I pressed my hand into my brows, thinking. "So then you followed me to The Guild?"

One bark, the hellhound's tongue sloshed out the side of his large mouth, making him look like a blown up version of a cartoon.

"So are you like a protective beast of some sort?"

One bark.

"Do you protect others besides me?"

Silence.

I wracked my brain, trying to think of a way to ask him why while remaining within the yes/no paradigm. Still, I couldn't deny the fear that started to creep into my body. Looking up into warm, amber eyes, I opened and shut my mouth several times searching for the right words to ask. "You were born in the other realm?"

One bark

"Does this mean I'm evil? If you were sent to watch over me?" If guardian angels in human folklore watched over the good, it seemed only logical that hellhounds watched over the bad. But my question was met with silence, and I exhaled in relief. Nothing about this overgrown dog screamed evil. "Did you get caught on purpose?" He was much too powerful and agile to make it easy for protectors to catch him. He'd taken on a werewolf and vampire, for crying out loud.

One bark.

I smiled, feeling somehow lighter that I had a not-so-scary hellhound watching my back. "I'll find a way to get you out of here. I can feel it in my bones that you aren't evil, no matter what kind of creature you are or where you come from." My fingers stroked lightly against the glass wall, as if I could pet him from here. "Do you have a name?"

Silence.

I smiled. Every dog should have a name. "Okay, let's find you one. Let me know when you come across one you like?" He barked once in response. "Fido?" Silence. "Riggs?" Silence. "Bruiser?" Silence. "Ralph?" One bark. I smiled, my teeth gleaming in the reflection of the glass. "Alright then, hellhound. We'll call you Ralph."

A deep throaty laughter from behind me had my heart beating something fierce—a sound that somehow both scared and enticed me.

I turned my head, but saw no one in the room. Ralph growled in response to my fear, the sound low and haunting.

I searched all around, trying to find the source of the sound, but every room was dark besides Ralph's sterile little prison. I wondered, briefly, if Greta had left a light on in his cage, anticipating that I'd come find him. I seriously owed that woman. Maybe I'd send her a fruit basket or something. Like a really big one, covered in chocolate.

"I can't believe you've named a hellhound. And that you've named it Ralph." The disembodied voice was low and deep and smooth, and I shuddered despite my fear.

In the room across from Ralph's, a dark, imposing figure slowly made its way towards me, stopping just as it reached the glass that wasn't glass. The glow from Ralph's room reached a bit, and I could make out more and more of the mysterious creature, the closer it stepped into the light.

I held back a gasp. This wasn't a creature, this was a man. And a beautiful one at that. Light, tousled blond hair framed an angular face. He was tall and built with lean muscle. But it was his eyes that had me captivated—they didn't quite match. His right eye was a mottled gold, the left a dark brown. Watching my appraisal he lifted the left side of his lips in a smirk.

"What are you?" I asked. The options were limitless. Incubus, werewolf, vampire, or some less common demon that I'd never heard of before. Cyrus wasn't big on explaining our world beyond 'kill, decapitate, stab.' And truthfully, his approach worked on all creatures, didn't matter the specific species.

Something about the glint in the man's eye, the lazy posture, and the confidence he exuded, despite being locked in a glorified cage, told me that this man—thing—was dangerous.

Instead of answering, he tilted his head, not unlike a cat, and stared at my neck. Feeling self-conscious, I pressed my fingers to the bandaged skin, while Ralph growled a soft, threatening warning behind me.

"You've been recently tasted, I see." He continued his watchful stare, making me feel like I was the one being studied behind a glass wall. His lips stretched into a terrifying caricature of a smile. I felt my heartbeat increase its heavy drum. "And survived. How interesting."

"My wound is covered, how can you possibly know what caused it?" I asked. I rolled my shoulders softly, cognizant of my injured arm, and squared my body for a fight. Which was probably a bit silly since this man was trapped somewhere he couldn't reach me. And while I was confident in my abilities, I wasn't deluded enough to think that I stood a chance against him, not solo, and definitely not in my current state.

He shrugged, cocking a single eyebrow. "There were others in here discussing an attack earlier. I saw the bandage on your neck and put two and two together. Your response confirmed it. They mentioned the fight was tonight. If that's true, I'm not quite sure how you're walking about and sneaking around right now." He sat down and crossed his legs, watching me like I was a favorite television program. His lazy perusal had my blood running cold.

What was he? Despite my fear, I couldn't deny that I was drawn to him. I couldn't look away, no matter how hard I tried. An incubus then?

"I wasn't bitten," I remarked, briefly recalling the concern on Cyrus's face. There was a reason I wasn't meant to discuss the attack with outsiders. Especially not evil ones locked in a creepy dungeon. "This," I touched my neck, "is just a cut. Ralph saved me before the fanghole had a chance to dig in."

"Whatever you say, little protector. Curious that you survived, all the same." His eyes danced briefly to Ralph before refocusing on me. "And perhaps more interesting, you've gained the companionship of a hellhound. It's rare for their kind to become familiars."

"Familiar?" My voice was soft and wispy. "You mean like a witch's familiar?" I asked, recounting the old story books I used to read when Cyrus wasn't hounding me to train or study up on more practical pursuits. As far as I knew, witches weren't real.

The man's grin deepened, somehow making him appear more

lethal. "No, not like a witch. Witches are merely humans with a few parlor tricks they've stolen or bought—nothing a familiar would ever waste their time on. Familiars never take a protector. But this one has. And a hellhound, no less. Why is that, little protector?"

Uncomfortable with his proximity, despite the glass protection, I backed into Ralph's wall. "You have a Hannibal Lecter thing going for you, you know that?" I tried to force as much confidence into my voice as I could muster. It wasn't much. "What are you?"

He laughed, and I caught my breath at the sound, at the look of the dangerous man with a beautiful smile. "You have fire, for such a small and young protector. I can almost pretend to understand why the hellhound, Ralph as you call him, has claimed you. You hold a certain fascination uncommon amongst your kind. His attachment must either be a very good omen, or a very, very bad one—I wonder which it is." His head tilted, his smile widened, and I watched in fascination as his canine teeth extended into two sharp fangs. I cringed, the memory of the last vamp I'd faced too fresh in my mind.

My lips turned in disgust. "Oh, you're one of them." I let myself feel briefly satisfied that the vamp was locked up in the middle of a research lab. The whole species deserved to be eradicated. His lips thinned into a tight, mocking smile while I turned back to the hellhound. I was no longer interested in entertaining his cellmate. "I'll try and see you again tomorrow, Ralph. Cyrus and Seamus assured me that no one will harm you while you're here—they are just keeping you locked up for preventative measures and appearances. My brother and I are already brainstorming ways to get you out as soon as we can."

Ralph barked once, licking the surface of the window that aligned with my cheek.

"Until tomorrow, then, little protector." The vampire's voice followed me out, taunting and chilly.

Maybe I could convince Cyrus to give Ralph a better neighbor.

Then again, maybe it was good for Ralph to keep an eye on the vampire—something about the knowing look in his mismatched eyes had me on edge.

I was probably just rattled from my first and last encounter with a vampire.

Quick and silent on my feet, I made it back to my bed without incident, hiding Greta's card key inside my pillowcase for safe keeping. I'd have to sneak it out with me when I was discharged.

I'd been at The Guild for a little over a day and I'd already encountered two vamps and a hellhound—at least living here wouldn't be dull. As I drifted off to sleep, my hazy brain focused on a pair of mismatched, arrogant eyes.

12

ATLAS

"We shouldn't have come here, Seamus." There was a brief pause before the voice, Cyrus I assumed from the grumbling tone, picked back up again. "I thought it was a good idea. But now—we've been here for a day and she's already almost been killed. I could have hidden her somewhere else, she needs more time."

I stood frozen outside of Seamus's place, uncomfortable with eavesdropping, but unwilling to pass up the chance to learn more about the Bentley family. After we left the infirmary, Seamus asked for me to meet with him. Most likely he wanted me to brief him again on what happened outside of Vanish.

And I didn't blame him. We needed to strategize. This was uncharted territory.

Vamps so close to Guild Headquarters? It was completely unheard of. And the fact that they actively attacked one of our own? Things were amping up a lot more than we realized.

"Cy, what's done is done. Outside of you and me, no one knows anything, okay. We can keep her safe. She needs training, and she needs to learn about our world. Eli and his team, they're trustworthy. I've known them all since they were kids. And I am telling you that there is no group better for her to learn from. They'll watch her back and keep her safe."

I bristled as he mentioned our team. Were the Bentleys the reason we were tapped to tackle teaching while Alleva was gone? I pinched my lips together and took a long breath in and out. The lack of information was grating. Seamus brought them here and now the girl was already under my team's skin. The way they all crowded around her bed, waiting for her to wake up. We had other things to focus on, other things to accomplish. Our timeline was crunching and having her here, getting in our heads, was not part of the plan.

"You've been doing her a disservice trying to ignore this," Seamus continued. "I spoke with Reese this afternoon and she said Max and Ro were almost completely clueless."

"I had my reasons—"

"Your reasons were selfish, don't pretend otherwise." Seamus let out a frustrated sigh. "You love her like a daughter. And you weren't planning on that. I get it. I'm shocked as hell, but I get it. I'm a parent too. But what she needs from you is not parental affection. It's going to get her killed. She needs to understand what she's up against. And soon. She's almost nineteen."

What the hell was she up against? It took every ounce of strength I had not to break the door down and demand answers.

"You don't know what you're talking about," Cyrus said, his voice picking up in volume.

I calmed my breathing as much as I could, hoping they couldn't hear me through the thin walls. The heavy wind was working in my favor, but their hearing was almost as good as mine. And snooping on my bosses was the exact opposite of what I should be doing right now.

"She's undisciplined, Cy, reckless. Look at this." There was a brief pause, and I heard some clunking around on the other side of the door.

"So what? So she went to see the hound." Cyrus let out an

exasperated chuckle and slammed something heavy down on a table. "To tell you the truth, I can't say I blame her."

"And you honestly think this is going to be a one-time thing? I've known the girl less than forty-eight hours and I know for certain she'll be back. I've erased this from the video feed for now but I can't keep her off the radar if she's downstairs having conversations with these creatures. She's going to draw attention. Even more than she already has."

What kind of attention were they so afraid of? I mean I understood why Cyrus was a bit frustrated. One of his kids had almost died, but this was something else. Who exactly was Max Bentley? And did they really think that someone or something was after her? Was it because of the wolf attack the other night, or something else?

I wiped my clammy hands against my jeans, taking deep, calming breaths. More than anything, I wanted Max Bentley away from here, away from us. She was drawing too much attention to herself and drawing my team into whatever problems and shadows followed her.

I counted to five before clearing my throat and loudly knocking on the door. Neither of them were obtuse, but hopefully they didn't suspect I heard too much.

"Come in," Seamus called, his voice raised louder than it had been, but still filled with a frustrated and exhausted edge.

I walked into Seamus's quarters to find both brothers studying me. Matching dark hair, matching dark eyes. Seated like this, the resemblance between them was uncanny. They were almost twins. I hadn't known Cyrus long, but it was still obvious to me that Seamus was the more jovial one between them. Not tonight though. There was a somberness to his expression, the lines around his mouth etched deeper than usual.

Not wanting to drag any dirt in, I tapped each boot roughly on the ground a few times before entering. "You er, wanted to see me sir? I hope I'm not interrupting anything important. I can come back later if it would be better for you."

I half hoped he'd take me up on it. After the intense evening, I wanted nothing more than a cold beer and a solid night's sleep. Plus Cyrus was looking at me like he wanted to peel back my skin, just to see what was under it. There weren't many protectors I found intimidating, but Cyrus Bentley was definitely one of them.

"Cy, this is Atlas. I don't think you've formally met him yet, especially not tonight with all of the chaos, but he's part of Six— the leader of Eli's group." Seamus ran a hand through his dark hair, frowning as his fingers got caught in a few tangles.

"Nice to meet you, sir." I stood up a bit straighter, not wanting to give either of them a reason to study me too closely.

Cyrus didn't respond, or even gesture in acknowledgement. His cold, depth-filled eyes just studied with me scrutiny.

Seamus coughed out a chuckle before turning back to me. "Sorry son, you'll have to excuse my brother. Rough night and all, with his kid." He backhanded Cyrus in the arm, hard enough to earn his brother's focus. "Atlas is a good kid. And he's got a hell of a team on his hands. I'd say the same, even if my son weren't on it. They'll take good care of Max, keep an eye on her."

"She's slippery." Cyrus let out a gruff groan, his arms crossed in front of his chest as he leaned back in his chair. His eyes softened slightly, just for a moment. "I don't care if you put the best this place has to offer on her tail, even I have difficulty keeping her out of trouble. And I have no reason to trust a bunch of kids I don't even know." He narrowed his eyes slightly, whatever warmth was there before was now nowhere in sight. "Same goes for your son. I see the way he looks at women—at her."

Of course. Eli was always sticking his dick where it didn't belong. And now Cyrus was going to be watching us extra close because of it. Great.

Seamus wasn't really the eye-rolling type, but the head-tilt thing he did was as close as it got. "The boys are the ones who found her and brought her back, Cy. Stop being so stubborn." As if suddenly remembering that I was still in the room, Seamus turned towards me and grinned. "Atlas, as I'm sure you're aware, brothers are a goddamn headache. But the reason I called you here tonight is to see if I can have you and the guys—Declan too, of course—keep an eye out for Max. This is the second time she's been attacked this week, and with the increase in supernatural activity, we don't want to take any chances."

"Of course." I gave him a small nod before glancing quickly at Cyrus again. He was back to studying me, his expression completely unreadable. "We can spend more time patrolling Guild boundaries. It's strange to have a vampire in our territory. Any word yet on what it was doing here?"

Seamus frowned, shaking his head. "No news. And while patrolling is appreciated as always, I was hoping that you could keep an eye on her in a more direct sense. I don't want her leaving campus, without one of you with her at all times. And I'd like for you to take her under your wing in terms of training—"

I opened my mouth to protest, but Seamus continued on, ignoring me.

"I know she's quite advanced, but she is also incredibly inexperienced. I understand that your brother is going to cover some extra tutoring sessions, which is great. I'd appreciate the rest of you looking out for her as well. She's family and I want her transition into this life to go as smoothly as possible."

I fought to keep my expression blank as my stomach sank. The last thing any of us needed right now was to play babysitter to a fucking puppy who had no idea how to function around people, let alone one who was a magnet for trouble.

"Er, sir," I started, trying to sound as gracious as possible. "I'm glad you thought of us, but are you sure that we're really the best option? Wouldn't it be better for her to work with one of the older, more advanced teams?"

Or, better yet, go back to wherever she came from?

"I think she'll fit in better with you. Especially since your team is in charge of training sessions for the next few days, until Alleva gets back. You're the natural choice."

I turned to Cyrus, hoping he would at least agree with me, but I was met with his persistent, impenetrable stare.

"Our field missions—" I started, trying to string together an argument. Any argument.

"Your assignments are significantly lightened, for as long as you are training, so it shouldn't be too big of a problem. And for the few days we need you and your team elsewhere, we can make something work." Seamus stood, stretching his neck. It had been a long night for all of us. "Don't worry, Atlas. Max is a good kid, I can tell. I'm sure we'll get all of this sorted eventually, it's just a temporary favor." He paused a moment, his muscles tense. "But please do be discreet about it. Can't have anyone getting upset about nepotism and worrying Max is getting preferential treatment."

I bit back my smirk. No one who grew up with Eli could ever accuse The Guild of giving preferential treatment to relatives of prominent members. Seamus made sure of that. If anything, Eli had a harder time than most, constantly under his father's scrutiny.

"Sir," I said quietly. With a reluctant nod, I acknowledged the assignment for exactly what it was—a decision outside of my control. And if Seamus was putting an entire team of protectors on Max detail, one thing was certain: there was far more to her than any of us realized. Maybe this would be my best chance to get to the bottom of it.

Until we learned why the hell Seamus and Cyrus were so hellbent on coddling her and keeping her under Guild radar, Max Bentley could not be trusted. And, I realized, my stomach hardening at the thought, maybe Seamus and Cyrus weren't to be trusted either.

❦ 13 ❧

MAX

For the next several days, I was locked in my suite like a prisoner while I healed. Only the thing was, I felt great. Even better than before the attack. Greta checked my vitals and found that I was perfectly fine, but Cyrus and Ro wanted me in bed just to be sure—it was an abnormal amount of blood to lose, and I'd certainly never been injured to quite that degree in our sparring sessions. Not to mention the three broken bones in my right arm and hand. Those took the longest to heal, and put me in the most amount of pain. One of the bones didn't heal quite right and had to be reset by Greta, leaving her to snicker at my tirade of swear words. She and I had a love-hate thing going on. Before I left, she loudly complained about having lost her ID card and what a pain it was to get a new one issued. The wink she immediately delivered, settled any fears I had about keeping her old one.

While it was nice that Ro delivered all my favorite foods to my bed, I was antsy and ready for a prison break. It was a special kind of torture, remaining on bed rest when my body felt like it was on an energy high. And I couldn't do anything about it, because after one failed escape attempt, I lost all privacy privilege—Cyrus and Ro kept watch over me in shifts, both of them hovering anxiously around my room like mother hens.

I had a feeling it had more to do with the "what if's" running through their minds, than the actual outcome of the attack. Not to mention they both kept shooting me furtive glances, eyes roving over the skin that no longer showed any evidence of housing vamp fangs. And according to Ro, the attack was all anyone could talk about.

"You're the talk of The Guild, Max. No one your age has ever lived to talk about a solo vamp win." Ro grinned, his eyes following my expression with amusement. We both knew that the only reason I survived was because of Ralph. Outside of the Alpha Six team and us, no one was allowed to know about him or give him the credit. Apparently hellhounds were a big deal, and if everyone found out that one was being housed underground here, I wouldn't be the only one breaking in to get a visit.

Which left me restless in a bed and a celebrity under false pretenses.

"Shut up. Did Cy go down to Ralph yet? Make sure he's doing okay? I told him I'd try to visit again and you jerks haven't given me the opportunity to." Ro's eyebrows turned in and his cheeks blushed. I frowned, guilt churning in my gut. "Sorry, I didn't mean to take that out on you. I'm just getting restless and the more I sit here all day, the more I think about how ridiculous it is that The Guild is keeping the hero of the story locked up in a glorified prison next to a creepy vamp. It's not exactly a great way to say thank you, is it? Can't we at least find him a nicer neighbor?"

Cyrus pushed through the door and entered my room. I'd conned Ro into letting me organize it a bit while I was 'resting.' Unlike Cyrus, Ro caved a little under pressure.

"I saw your hellhound." Cy's voice was gruff, while his eyes took in the changes to my room. They were small—I'd repositioned the bed against the wall, moved the dresser a few inches to the left so that the window wasn't blocked, and a few smaller things—but Cyrus noticed everything immediately, and I grinned when I saw his expression catalogue that the rug was moved over half an inch. Ro and I did that just to see if he'd notice. Both of our lips tightened in amusement, but neither of us was willing to mock Cyrus openly.

"His name is Ralph, Cy. I keep telling you that." At his answering eye roll, I jumped to the end of my bed, excited for news. "Well, did you talk to him? What did he say? Is he okay? They haven't hurt him have they? I'll kill anyone that tries. When can I go down there?"

Cyrus shook his long mane of hair out in frustration. "You don't name a hellhound, Max," he said, pausing as his annoyance bled into amusement. "And if you do, you don't name him Ralph."

"Hey, he chose it, not me. I thought it only fair that at least one of us got a choice in our names."

"First of all, your name is perfectly nice, Maxi—'

I cut him off with a hiss, while he crossed over to sit on the small chair Ro had just abandoned.

"Second, hellhounds don't talk."

I looked up at him, smug. "Mine does." Ro raised an eyebrow at me and I dropped my shoulders. "Okay, he doesn't say, like, words or anything. But we have a system. And he can understand what I'm saying."

"Unlikely, I've never met any creature who understands what she's saying," Cyrus muttered not-so-covertly to Ro. The pair of them shared a chuckle at my expense. It was fine, I was used to it. And I secretly enjoyed being their source of amusement. Life got boring in the cabin if we didn't do all we could to liven it up a bit. Family was a weird thing.

"I know what I saw. Ralph chose Ralph and he understood what I said to him. But if you want to mock, fine. Moving on to the next question, then. How is he and have they done anything to him down there?"

"He's perfectly fine," Cyrus answered before shooting an

amused look over at Ro. "And apparently very pleased that Ro threatened one of the guards until they agreed to give him a couple of steaks last night."

I grinned proudly at Ro before turning back to Cyrus. We'd both bugged Cy for years to let us get a pet. This was the closest we'd ever come to actually having one. "What about the vamp, did they find anything weird in his venom or whatever? Because not only are my fang holes gone, but I feel absolutely great."

His dark brows furrowed and his usually tan skin paled a few shades. "No, nothing unusual in his venom or teeth—" he paused, shifting his focus between us, "Seamus and I were serious the other night, you can't go telling people about the bite until we know more."

I had a feeling that Izzy would get me to spill as soon as she was granted visitation rights though. I'd known her for all of a day and she was already my favorite person after Ro and Cyrus.

I let out a breath of air, puffing my hair to the side. "No kidding. I'm already going to be such a freak here now, I don't need to go looking for more reasons. Was probably just a freak thing. Or maybe Ralph healed me somehow? He licked the wound after I killed the vamp." I paused a moment, thinking. "Come to think of it, he slobbered on me after the wolf attack too. Maybe hellhound saliva has healing properties. The creepy vamp downstairs told me Ralph was connected to me some—"

"I don't want you speaking to that vampire again, Max. I'm neither naive nor obtuse enough to think you won't be down there to visit that dog again, but you're to ignore anything else you see down there. The beasts and demons downstairs are both intelligent and dangerous."

Demons? They had demons down there? Demons were real?

I shook my head, trying to maintain focus. I was still working on the whole hellhounds were real thing and, right now, that took precedence.

Cyrus stood up quickly and dropped a heavy tote on my bed. "Now read up, you have a lot to catch up on before you get back to your classes tomorrow. I'm sure Ro can confirm that this academy here is no joke and you're both already very far behind. I've kept you from this world long enough, but since you seem to be running towards it, and it towards you, with all the grace of a troll, you need to catch up." Cy moved towards my door before looking back at me. "And some infernal girl keeps pestering me for details about your recovery everywhere I turn. Her phone number is listed on several pieces of paper in that bag. Update her yourself and tell her if she bugs me again, I'll make her training a living hell."

And with that he was gone.

"I'm going to go pick up some dinner. I'll bring you back a plate," Ro said before following him out.

I rummaged through the bag, ignoring all of the heavy books and pulled out the number so I could give Izzy a call. My body was humming with excitement about getting back to classes and exploring the academy before I looked at the absurd number of assignments I had to make up. This was going to be a long night. I'd have to bribe Ro into helping me later on.

I NEVER THOUGHT I'D BE SO EXCITED TO GO TO SCHOOL.

Okay, okay, that was a lie. I'd begged Cy for years to let me go to a real school, with real people. But I was even more excited today than I had been when we first arrived. After throwing on some brand new workout clothes that Izzy left outside my door as a get-well present, I was ready for my jailbreak. The leggings were black and had grey swirls, and the top was a strappy black sports bra. I threw on a black zip up to cover up. I wasn't exactly comfortable with wandering around campus with so much skin showing.

"Jesus, Max, chew your food before you swallow it," Ro said, staring at my plate. It was already half empty before he even had a chance to sit down and join me. "It's not going to run away from you or anything. Plus, if you eat that fast, you'll be sick during training this afternoon. And after so many days of rest, it's bound to be a difficult session as it is."

"Cy said last night that if I hurry up, he'll let me down to feed Ralph some breakfast." I nodded to the large pile of eggs, sausage, and ham sitting on the plate next to mine. "I'm hoping to trick him into letting me take him for a bit of a walk so he can stretch his legs. His little window room was tiny." I shivered, thinking about how claustrophobic I'd been feeling over the last few days, and I had a whole suite to myself. If he was anything like me, he was seriously struggling down there.

"He's not a pet, Max."

Declan's voice startled me enough that I dropped my fork and had to pause the food-to-mouth shoveling process I'd perfected. Craning my neck, I found her standing above me, dressed head-to-toe in black and looking every part the avenging angel. She seemed so serious, and standoffish, even now when there was a hint of teasing in her tone. Out of everyone I'd met, she was the most difficult person here for me to get a read on—and that was even including Atlas and his consistent dickishness.

"I know he's not a pet," I answered, sliding my tongue over my teeth to make sure there wasn't food stuck somewhere. "But he did save my life. Twice. And he deserves to be treated decently, especially since I'm the reason he's cooped up in the first place."

She rolled her teeth over her bottom lip, her pink tongue peeking out just briefly. She seemed to be weighing something and after a moment of internal struggle, landed on a decision. "Fair enough. I saw Cyrus outside. How about I come with you to greet the hellbeast? I didn't get to meet him the night of the, er, event."

I breathed out in surprise and grabbed the pile of food I'd scavenged for Ralph. "Awesome, let's go now. Ro, you in?" I turned back to him.

He nodded once before bussing my tray and joining us. I

could get used to him waiting on me. Maybe getting attacked by a vampire came with a few perks.

Now that food didn't have my complete attention, I noticed everyone's eyes trained on me, with whispers trailing every table we passed. I scratched at the invisible bite on my neck, uncomfortable with the attention. Luckily it was early, so the room was fairly empty. Declan opened the main doors as we reached them, scowling at a group of students who were debating rather loudly whether or not I was actually attacked by a vampire or just making the whole thing up for attention.

I recognized Theo and Reza in the center of the group and suppressed a groan. As if the attention wasn't bad enough—now I had to worry about people thinking I was asking for it.

"Ignore them," Ro muttered, while Declan shot over an icy look that shut them up instantly. I'd have to learn that trick sometime. My intimidation factor was apparently really low.

Ignore them. I knew that was the mature thing to do, that I shouldn't care what people thought of me. But that was a lot easier said than done. I opened my mouth to defend my honor when the sight of Cyrus had me snapping it closed again.

Right. Ralph. That was way more important. Maybe ignoring them would be easier than I'd thought.

"Cy!" I entered into a light jog, balancing the plate of food precariously. Ro and Declan trailed right behind me. Cyrus looked more tired than usual, a weariness on his face that I wasn't used to. The bags under his eyes were the sort of heavy they got after a night of hard drinking. Which, to be fair, happened regularly. Cyrus had more demons than most, that much was evident. Even if I had no clue what any of them were. "Can I go see Ralph before my sessions start for the day? It's been ages. I promised I'd try to visit him days ago."

I sounded like a whiny child. I heard it. I was aware. I just also, in this moment, didn't really care. My body was humming with energy.

Cyrus pinched the bridge of his nose, frustration flaring

briefly behind his eyes. "No you can't. Not now, Max. I'm sorry. Just focus on your courses and training for the moment. And take it easy. It's your first day back."

"But—" I started, stumbling at the exhaustion crawling across his features. Had he gotten any sleep? "You said I could visit him, that you'd try to get me in. Why can't I just go right now?" I turned back towards the infirmary, ready to do just that.

"Max, he's not there right now," anger laced his voice but I realized instantly it wasn't directed towards me. The bend in his posture made him almost look sorry, guilty even.

"What's going on Cy?" Ro took a step next to me, squaring off in solidarity. His heavy hand clapped down on my shoulder, the reverberation enough to drop a piece of bacon from my plate.

Cyrus glanced briefly at Declan, a curious look passing over his face, like he was sizing her up, determining whether she was trustworthy or not. He turned back towards me. "They have him in a lab right now. They're running tests. Studying him. Seeing if they can get to the bottom of his fascination with you, along with the vampire. With the increased other realm activity, everyone is on high alert and every supernatural beast is viewed as hostile or suspicious until proven otherwise. It's the way things are in this world. I'm sorry. Maybe another day."

Anger like I'd never felt before bubbled low in my belly. "What the hell are you talking about?" My fingernails sunk deep into the cushions of my hands, as the plate dropped to the ground, splattering my shoes with runny eggs. "What kind of tests? Are they hurting him?"

"How did you let this happen?" Ro's temple was pulsing as he bent down to scoop the food back onto the plate. "Ralph is the whole reason Max is even alive right now. We owe him. How could you let them take him and run tests on him?"

"They wanted to put him down." Cy's eyes rose to meet ours. "If I didn't let them run their tests, they were going to kill him. Hellhounds are notoriously dangerous and unpredictable. You have no idea what kind of reputation and history they have amongst our people. It was the best way I could protect him. Trust me, I'm not happy about this situation. Not one bit. I didn't have much of a choice."

Declan scratched at the back of her neck, clearly uncomfortable. She exhaled softly, shaking her head. Dark strands of her hair spilled out of her ponytail and curled around her shoulder.

"Got something to add?" I snapped, a little too aggressively at her. The frustration in my voice made even me wince—but, for some reason, I couldn't completely contain it.

"This shouldn't have happened," she started, tentatively, "but I'm sure there's a good reason for this. They probably just want to make sure he's safe. See if there's anything they can learn about the other realm from him. I'm sure they're just trying to make sure that he doesn't hurt anyone, or at least try to figure out why he keeps showing up only when there's trouble."

The accusation buried in her voice made me bristle and Ro's fingers brushed over mine in a quiet warning. Too bad I was terrible at heeding those warnings. Especially now.

"What the hell is wrong with this place? How is this even a discussion?" I turned on Declan, unfazed by the tension in her jawline. I needed to let some of my frustration out. I felt like I was ready to explode at a moment's notice. Like the vampire's aggression was pooling in my blood along with his venom. "He's not some demon beast who's orchestrating attacks. He's a harmless dog who saved my life. How can you think this is even a little bit okay? Ralph is the whole reason I'm even alive right now. He shouldn't be in a cage in the first place, let alone subjected to who knows what down in your evil dungeon."

Guilt. I was feeling guilt. And while my brain could recognize it, I couldn't stop it from spewing out of my lips.

"That's not what—" Declan stuttered, looking down. Her nose flared slightly. "You're right. I'm sorry. You've been here all of ten seconds, so clearly you have this all figured out." She looked past me so that her green eyes landed on Cy. "Good to see you again, sir." With a shake of her head, she turned and left.

And of course, the very second that she left, shame pooled low in my belly. It wasn't her fault, I knew that. And I knew it wasn't Cy's fault either. My temper was all over the place today and I needed to sort it out before I snapped at someone else. I wasn't sure if it was the house arrest or the leftover effects of vampire saliva—gross—but my mood swings were on another level.

Without another word to Cy, I turned out of the cafeteria. It was early enough that I could still squeeze in a jog before my morning classes, or else the anger, frustration, and helplessness would cloud my mind and make training impossible. Ro stayed behind, which was good. He was always the best when it came to figuring out whether I needed space or company.

The breeze lapped against my skin as I tore through the east side of the forest. There were a few odd cabins scattered in this part of the grounds, but it was serene and devoid of anyone. Most people were probably still grabbing breakfast.

The isolated calm of crashing through the forest and hopping around overgrown tree roots did wonders for slowing down my thoughts and letting me assess the situation. Cyrus and Seamus made sure that Ralph wasn't put down. He was as safe as he could be, given the alternative. For now, I had to be thankful for that. It was a start.

So the next step was to find a way to get him out of here. I wasn't entirely sure why he let himself get captured like that, but regardless of the reason, he was not going to die here. I wouldn't let it happen. I could feel it in my bones that he didn't mean me harm, I just needed to find a way to prove it.

Almost a second too late, I realized that I was heading straight for a quaint little pond. Planting the brakes, I went skidding through the mud until I stopped an inch before the water.

"Shit," I breathed, hands planted on my knees as I caught my breath. I plopped down and started laughing as the cool breeze

dried away sweat. The sun was up now and it reflected beauti-
fully against the glassy water, the ripples dancing around the lily
pads and twigs from surrounding trees. Something about the
serenity here reminded me of home—of being far away, secluded.
The thoughts running through my brain, the fears, they seemed
to almost entirely stop.

"Beautiful isn't it?" a low voice sounded behind me.

I froze, tension spilling through my body as I turned, looking
for the voice. It was rare for me to be caught off guard like that.
Was I still within Guild boundaries? I needed to get a map asap.

And then I saw a familiar set of brown eyes. "Eli."

"The one and only," he said, walking over and dropping down
next to me. He picked up a rock and tossed it into the water,
creating a fresh wave of ripples across the surface. "This is my
favorite place on campus. I used to come here a lot to clear my
head. Not too shabby, right?"

The usually cocky, teasing expression on his face was softer
out here. He was still devastatingly good looking, but he seemed
more gentle in this light, less intimidating.

"Feeling better, kid? We were all pretty worried about you,"
he dropped his head down, his elbows bowed against his knees,
"after you know, the attack."

Trying not to bristle too much at the kid comment—after all,
I *had* been acting like a petulant child just a few moments ago—I
nodded. "Honestly, I feel pretty great."

His dark eyes turned towards me, studying the now smooth
spot of skin on my neck. He reached a hand forward, like he
wanted to trace the invisible mark with his finger, but dropped it
before reaching me.

"Amazing. When I brought you in—there was so much
blood. Your neck, it was a mangled mess." He shook his head, a
crease forming between his brows as he studied me. "I don't
understand how it's just gone now."

I shrugged, smiling awkwardly. There wasn't anything to say.
I didn't understand it either. And over the last few days, I forced

myself not to think about it, not to question it too closely. Because I wanted desperately to belong here, to belong to this world I'd only ever read about. This? The miraculously healing vamp attack? That was something that set me apart when I wanted so badly to fit in.

Clearing my throat, I met his eyes. "I'm sorry about that night—" I broke off, unsure how to handle this topic. Especially since the thought of Eli, pounding into the girl from the shop, coated me in an uncomfortable heat. I looked away, unable to match his stare any longer. "I didn't mean to, you know, interrupt. And I really should have left immediately, but shock just sort of had me frozen for a second too long." I could feel myself blushing, and I hoped that the evidence wasn't painted across my cheeks.

Eli laughed, a low rumbly sound before pressing his fingers into the ground and leaning back. His body had inched over closer to me, and I was all too aware of his energy surrounding me. "Don't worry about it. I'm sorry that I teased you about it. I made an already awkward situation worse." He snuck a few looks at me out of the side of his eye. "Forgiven?"

I nodded, unable to stop the grin. "I hope I didn't ruin things between you and that girl?" Judging by the sounds she was making when I left, she didn't exactly seem like she was in a grudge-holding mood.

"Who? Emily? No, she was fine. We laughed it off after you left and she's already contacted me for another date. So no harm, no foul."

For some reason, the thought of them having another date stung, but I brushed it off and grinned at him, glad that I hadn't messed things up too badly for him. "Is it difficult dating humans? Cy's always been really strict about letting us around them for too long. And the one time I got close, the protector world just—complicated things."

Poor Michael. I hoped wherever he was, he was okay now. And hopefully concussion-free. Though I had a feeling that his brother was quite pleased that we'd moved away in the middle of the night.

Eli's eyes widened as he straightened his spine. "Oh, I don't *date* humans, Max. None of us do. Hook up? Yes. Anything more than that? Hell no. Way too complicated and way too dangerous, for everyone involved."

Right, that made sense, although I wasn't sure if I could really do the whole casual thing. Especially since my experience was exactly one fishy kiss and nothing more. My thoughts floated to the conversation in class my first day. "Is your mate okay with that?" He made a weird choking sound and I belatedly realized that was absolutely none of my business. "Sorry, that was way too nosy of me. Please don't answer."

"My. Mate." He looked off over the water, his brows bent in confusion. "What makes you think I have a mate?"

My stomach dropped and I dug my fingers into the dirt, trying desperately to disappear from this conversation. "Er, sorry. I just remember my lesson from the other day. Reese—I think that was her name—was talking about bondmates and protectors. And then you'd mentioned the Headmistress's bondmates before, so I just assumed—that everyone had one once they were placed in teams?"

A giant grin stole across his face as he shook his head softly, breathing out an incredulous chuckle. "No Max, I don't have a mate. And even if I did, they aren't inherently romantic or sexual. I think you've maybe been watching too many movies and reading too many romance novels. I'll probably end up bonded to Dec eventually, but it will be for a way to strengthen our team, nothing more. We'll both be free to, er, go after our own individual pursuits." He paused, studying me again as he scratched his cheek. The expression in his eyes was unreadable, but I shivered nonetheless. "Cyrus really kept you both in the dark, didn't he."

It wasn't a question, more so an acknowledgment.

I nodded, not sure what more I could add. I seemed to be

digging myself in deeper and deeper here. And the more I fell into this world, the more I questioned why Cy had hidden so much of it from us. It certainly made our entry into The Guild unnecessarily confusing.

He brushed my shoulder playfully with his. "Allow me to demystify then. Bonds are sacred to us. They strengthen trust between team members, and act as a sort of vow. Sometimes they become more than that. But that's all they are. When two or more protectors—or, more realistically, their parents—decide to bond together, there's a ceremony and the ties are woven. It's a strange magic our kind has fabricated over the years. True bonds were a part of our history, they occurred naturally. But that hasn't happened in centuries—maybe it never even happened at all, realistically." He paused, skipping another rock. We both watched in silence until the pebble and waves slowly disappeared. "Over the years, the bonds have functioned as a tradition, nothing more. A way to keep us safe in a life that can be quite dangerous. So yes, you'll most likely be tied to another protector one day, but that doesn't have to mean anything more than loyalty and friendship."

I let his words wash over me and I felt the tension slipping away, morsel by morsel. Put this way, I could almost understand why the ritual was so highly revered in this community. The thought of someone always there, to have my back, was...nice.

"Then again, a lot of times, the bonds are chosen as a way to create ideal pairings for future generations. It really just depends on how you, your bondmate, and your guardians view the situation."

Just like that, the serenity washing over me shattered. I narrowed my eyes at him, which solicited another chuckle.

"You're cute when you pout," he said, his smile melting away as he stood up and cleared his throat. "Come on, we should go. Don't want you to be late for your first day back. It's sure to be a rough one." He held out his hand and I grabbed it, my skin tingling as he pulled me to my feet. As if burned, he dropped my hand as soon as I was stable. "Do me a favor, Max? This place is pretty important to me. You're welcome out here anytime you need a place to reflect, or whenever you need a few minutes of solitude. But don't go talking about it. This place will lose its magic if everyone knows it exists."

I nodded, waiting for him to lead the way back. He had nothing to worry about. While I'd found this place on my own, the odds of me finding it again, let alone describing the directions to somebody, were almost impossible. And if I didn't have him to help me retrace my steps, who knows if I would've ever found my way back to the path.

❧ 14 ❧
MAX

After a morning of classes, my excitement for rejoining the campus activities considerably dwindled. I sat through three hours of lectures that focused on dissecting the battle strategies of a specific werewolf pack from the eighties—using terminology that might as well have been elvish for all I could understand of it.

And this lesson took place all while fielding suspicious glances and less-than-quiet discussions about the vamp attack outside of Vanish. The teachers were all on high alert and I could practically feel the overpowering sense of doom and fear layered heavily in the air. This was the furthest a vampire had ever crossed into protector territory. Students were banned from leaving the campus without team supervision until further notice, and instructors who lived away from the school were temporarily staying in some of the empty cabins scattered around the grounds.

Between the gossip surrounding my near death, the anxiety coating the atmosphere, and the situation with Ralph, I was less than enamored with life in The Guild my first day back. Part of me even wanted to escape back into my cave of an apartment, shunning everyone but Ro, Cy, and Izzy. But at least we had training in the afternoon. Kicking ass was one of the best ways to melt away any of the lingering frustration.

I ducked when Eli's fist came flying lazily towards me. I dug my nails into my palm and swept his feet so that he went tumbling down hard on the mat. The resounding thud of his back against the spongy material didn't bring the usual excitement of a win with it. He was my third sparring partner of the day.

Wade was even more hesitant to fight me than he had been on my first day. And he'd spent most of the afternoon session off scowling in annoyance for being called out once again by his brother. Declan didn't have much better luck.

While my frustration with her over our Ralph discussion fueled my fight, it seemed to have the opposite effect on her; her moves were more predictable than they were the first time we fought, and I could see her annoyance with me clouding her judgment. I was partially convinced that she threw the fight so that Atlas would let her go spar with someone else. Part of me knew I needed to apologize for snapping at her, I just wasn't sure how.

Eli's half-assed performance was somewhere in the middle of the two, but I could tell he was holding back, like he didn't think I was ready to get back to fighting just yet. And that infuriated me.

"You didn't even try," I mumbled, as he stared up at me with a sheepish grin. I grabbed his forearm and hoisted him back up until he was towering over me again.

After surviving a vamp attack, you'd think I would have proven myself as a worthy protector and adversary, not some fragile little flower.

"Not sure what you're talking about," he shrugged, that annoying almost-smile plastered across his face again.

I breathed in deeply, knocking him back on the ground almost as soon as he'd regained his footing. I wasn't feeling weak. In fact, I felt stronger and more awake to the fight than I had before being attacked. It was almost like the vamp's bite had supercharged me or something. When I'd mentioned it to Ro and Cyrus, they told me I was being ridiculous, had seen way too many superhero movies, and to not go spreading that kind of crap around to everyone. Which was fine with me—I was already getting more attention today than I wanted, I didn't need to go around bragging that I was becoming the vampire version of Spiderman. Which I guess was just...a vampire?

Momentary panic clouded my senses. I ran my tongue along my teeth. No sharp points. I hadn't had any cravings for blood either. I exhaled.

Of course, I knew that protectors couldn't be turned into vampires, but the fear was still there—like when you read up about your sore throat on WebMD and walked away suddenly convinced you were dying of some rare cancer.

"Eli, get up. This is getting ridiculous." Atlas walked over for the third time today, sizing me up, a look of annoyance driving lines between his dark, always-angry eyebrows. "She's not going to get any better if everyone gives her special treatment. Go spar with Rowan."

Eli blew out a breath of frustration, mumbling to himself about Atlas having a stick up his ass as he walked over to Ro. I watched for a minute as he got into position, and narrowed my eyes when, almost immediately, he was back to fighting like his typical self. Within a few maneuvers, he had Ro pinned and yielding. Shaking my head, I caught sight of Declan. I saw her nostrils flare in frustration briefly, like she knew I was watching her, but she refused to make eye contact. Ignoring me, she walked over to coach Izzy and Reza through their match up. I watched as Izzy landed a killer jab into Reza's side, unable to stop the grunt of approval from leaving my lips. Izzy was a badass.

The sound of someone clearing their throat startled me back to my own little fighting ring. Atlas was still standing behind me, the realization of which had me backing up a few paces. He was...a lot to take in.

I tried to ignore the way his black t-shirt hugged his muscular chest. And I absolutely refused to think about how he would look without it. Because while Atlas was all kinds of pretty in that I-can-kill-you-without-even-trying sort of way, he was an asshole. And there was no way that I was going to let myself have lusty thoughts about a dude who treated me like a pile of dog shit that had ruined his brand new shoes.

"You done watching the show or can we get back to training?" he asked, his dark eyes cold and assessing.

"Er, what show?" I asked, my words hurried and awkward. Had he noticed me checking him out? The thought had me ready to melt into the ground with shame.

"Reza and Izzy," he said. He lifted a single dark brow and stared at me like I was completely dense. "You're here to work, not to spectate."

"Right." My jaw tightened and I looked around. "Who's my next sparring partner?"

"I am."

My mouth dried a bit. I hadn't spent any alone time with Atlas and any time I happened to meet his eyes or catch him watching me, he was always rocking a startling level of anger and hatred. It was annoying, having someone treat you like a mortal enemy or, at the very least, a nuisance, with no clear reason why.

"You?" I asked, my throat croaking slightly. The adrenaline that had been pumping through my body all day bled out of me in one go. I felt lethargic, nervous all of a sudden.

"Riveting conversation, let's just start, yeah?" He ran a bored hand through his thick hair as his eyes roamed around the gym. I had the feeling that he was watching every single fight at once— like he could dissect each match in elaborate detail without focusing on any one for longer than a second or two. In some ways, he was more intimidating than even Cyrus.

I took a few steps back and raised my arms, pushing my

center of gravity forward a bit. Not waiting for him to say anything more, I did as he asked and started. Moving quickly, I pretended to throw a punch, but instead ducked and tried sweeping his legs. The move had worked hundreds of times on Ro, but I didn't have the same luck with Atlas. He hopped over my leg immediately, as if he knew tripping him was my plan all along. I stood up and turned, catching his foot a few centimeters before it would've hit my chest. He was a lot heavier than me though, so despite my blocking most of the blow, the contact drew a brief gasp from my lips.

We continued for what felt like forever, matching each other move for move. Sweat caked my body and I could feel my hair sticking to my neck, as if I'd just gone for a swim. In fact, the promise of a swim filled me with wild envy right about now.

Any time I paused, thinking we'd get to take a quick water break with everyone else, I was met with another kick or punch. Atlas was relentless in a way that no opponent I'd ever faced had been. He was faster, stronger, and had more awareness of my every movement than anyone—even Cy. And Cy was the one who'd taught me all of my moves in the first place, so if anyone should've been able to read me, it was him. Hell, if Atlas wasn't giving me such a thorough ass kick right now, I would have been impressed.

Okay, okay, I was still impressed, I just would never admit it out loud. The cocky gleam in his eyes was proof enough that he could live without an ego boost.

After half an hour of nonstop attacks, my breath was pulling in heavy, embarrassing wheezes. I looked around the room, noticing that we were drawing a crowd. It appeared that everyone else was watching us, no longer focused on their own training. I could understand why. I'd watched Atlas spar before, and he was a sight to behold. Still, the scrutiny, or at least my sudden awareness of it, had my nerves bouncing chaotically. I wasn't used to having an audience. And if anyone wanted to know my opinion of the experience, I wasn't really a fan.

Then, all at once, I found myself no longer staring at the faces in the gym, my eyes studying the rather unremarkable ceiling instead. My body landed heavily on the mats, pulling a reluctant wheeze and groan from me. My sweat-coated skin sloshed unpleasantly against the weird plastic material and I was certain that when I stood up, there would be a disgusting sweat angel of my body.

Atlas had taken advantage of my momentary distraction, and I was seething with anger—frustrated with myself, with him, with the entire Guild and everything that had happened since we got here. How did I wake up this morning looking forward to a day of classes and training? Right now, I wanted nothing more than to curl up in our cabin with an old blanket and my Netflix account. Just for a moment, I wanted to have a regular family and be a regular human teenager at a normal human college. Slowly but surely, I was beginning to understand why Cyrus had spent so much of his life hidden away from this world. It was...a lot.

"Get up, Bentley," Atlas said, lips quirked up slightly in a mocking grin. There was that annoying arched brow again.

"I don't think I will, actually." I breathed in and out, allowing myself a few moments to catch my breath and steady my heart rate. I could hear every beat pounding in my ears.

"I said get up." Atlas glanced quickly around the rest of the gym before looking over at the clock on the wall. "Not sure why you're all standing around, there's still twenty minutes left."

I sat up, watching as everyone scattered, leaving Declan and Eli in our own personal audience. The heat of their stares boiled my last nerves. Their eyes danced from me to Atlas, like they were taking in the start of an entertaining new show.

"Now, Bentley." Atlas's words were clipped, terse.

I jumped up and felt all of the frustration of the day pool low into my belly until it just—snapped. "I'm sorry. Have I fucking done something to you? Made your life hell in another life? Kicked your puppy?"

Atlas narrowed his eyes, "what do you mean?"

"I mean that ever since I've gotten here, you've looked at me like I'm the spawn of Satan. Not sure what exactly I've done to deserve that. But either tell me what it is, or start treating me like you treat everyone else in this gym."

"I'm training you, there's nothing personal." His eyes narrowed as he took a step closer to me, then another.

I let out a frustrated chuckle, feeling like a caged animal. "Training me? You've trained with Ro and haven't been an absolute jerk to him. I've won most of my spars since I got to The Guild. It's my first day back after a vamp attack and I haven't had a break in almost an hour. So I'll ask again, is there a reason you're being such a dick?"

Atlas prowled a few steps closer towards me, the muscles in his jaw clenching in time with each step. There was something wild, unhinged even, in his eyes as he studied me unblinking.

"Easy Atlas," Eli muttered from the sidelines. "She's had a rough first week here. Let's just take a breather for a few minutes and then go again."

"Did the vamp go easy on you at Vanish?" Atlas asked, a hint of mocking anger lacing his words. "Did he stop when you were getting tired? Did he go easy on you when you were having trouble keeping up? I don't want to waste anyone's time training you if you're just going to function as supernatural bait and die." His voice was so soft, so quiet, I had to strain to hear each word. "If that's your goal, just let me know and you're free to go whenever and wherever the hell you want. I won't waste the resources or my time."

"Atlas," Declan said, moving a few inches closer to us. She stood in front of me, placing herself in Atlas's line of sight. She was tall enough that she eclipsed my view. "Don't. She's right. You're being a dick, even for you."

I felt a momentary flutter that even Declan was sticking up for me right now. And it was weirdly validating that I wasn't the only one who noticed how much of an asshat Atlas was being.

My heart beat heavily against my chest. I remembered the strength the vamp had, the way he had pinned me; remembered the fact that I would have been dead within two minutes if it weren't for Ralph finding me and taking over the fight.

And then, in a rush, I remembered the werewolf, and how Ralph had helped then too. I'd faced two supernatural creatures in the last week and survived both encounters through sheer luck. Because I had a fuzzy fairy godmother. And now Ralph was locked in a glorified dungeon, surrounded by who knows how many evil dudes. If I was going to help him escape, and if I was going to protect myself outside of these grounds, I needed to suck it up.

I squared my shoulders and stretched my neck from side to side, resolve sinking in low and heavy. Atlas—and the whole Guild in general, really—was wearing my patience thin today, but I needed to get over it. This was life and death, I wasn't in a protected cabin anymore. I wasn't here to be pampered. I had wanted to fight, to be a protector, for as long as I'd known what that was—no matter how much Cyrus tried to shield us from the realities of that life. And so far, that life wasn't like it was in the movies, all good parts and fun and badassery. It was work and frustration and toil and good parts mixed with the bad.

I didn't get to speed through my training montage, as much as I wanted to.

Besides, this whole stubborn brat thing was not a good color on me. I was here to learn, and if Atlas wanted to serve that lesson with a side of douche, I'd take it.

"You're right," I said, stepping around Declan to confront them both. The shock on their faces had me physically restraining from the urge to roll my eyes. "I want to learn how to defend myself against a vampire." I took a deep breath in and out, steadying my pulse and letting go of my pride. "But I also want to learn how to kill one."

Atlas nodded. "I can do that."

"And," I said, clearing my throat, and meeting his gaze, "I

want to learn how to kill a werewolf." I wasn't sure how much Cyrus had told The Guild about our time in the cabin, but I was starting to think that the increased presence of other realm creatures was a lot worse than anyone realized and that I was an unlucky creature magnet of some sort. Two run-ins in the span of one week wasn't anything to balk at.

Atlas's eyes hardened before breaking eye contact with mine. I turned to Declan and Eli, both of whom were studying Atlas. It was like the three of them were having a silent conversation, one that was layered with surprise and discomfort.

"Fine," Atlas said, resolve icing over his tone, "we can teach you that too."

Without another word or glance in my direction, Declan left to spar with Ro and Wade. Eli and Atlas spent the rest of the time teaching me how to utilize supernatural weaknesses as strengths. There weren't many, but it was pretty clear that vampires and werewolves were hyper focused on the scent of their prey. Thinking of myself as a poor defenseless bunny didn't exactly inspire confidence and power, but it did help me understand that most supernatural monsters would be underestimating me. I wasn't as strong as they were, but I was definitely stronger than the average human.

I flung the wooden staff at Atlas, grinning like a Cheshire when the wood met the skin of his neck with a dull 'thunk.'

"Decapitated!" I yelled, my words echoing around the room. I looked around, most everyone was gone except for Atlas, Eli, Ro, and Izzy. The latter of whom was snickering behind her hand.

Right, I guess that wasn't really the sort of thing people went around triumphantly yelling.

"Again," Atlas said, knocking the practice staff away from his head. "This time aim for the heart. If the autopsy of that vamp revealed anything, it's that you don't have the best aim."

I narrowed my eyes, frustrated by the comment, but didn't say anything. As much as I wished he was wrong, he was right.

"Dude, can't we go eat?" Ro asked, leaning against the wall. He was freshly showered and wearing a new pair of jeans. "Everyone else left half an hour ago. You're going to wear her out."

"Again," I said, echoing Atlas.

Ro groaned, but he gave up arguing. He knew how to tell the difference between when I was being stubborn but malleable, and when I was three shades past stubborn, in which case there was no hope. And this was the latter.

It took another twenty minutes before I landed a hit that would have pierced his heart, had I been using my full strength and not swinging a blunt weapon. Worst I could do with this glorified stick was bruise him for a few seconds or give him an annoying splinter.

The two of us met, entwined, unraveled, over and over again until I had trouble deciphering where my body ended and his began. We were both caked in sweat—even though I was pretty sure most of it was mine—our chests heaving with heavy breaths. Neither of us wanted to break, neither of us wanted to give in to the other.

My eyes met his, temporarily entrancing me as I watched gold bleed into brown. I licked my lips, suddenly aware of how very close we were—how there was nothing more than a thin layer of fabric blocking my chest from his.

A low, guttural growl built up in his chest and for a moment I half thought he might grab me in the way a man grabs a woman, not in the way two fighters embrace. The moment slipped away as soon as it came. Feeling foolish, I took advantage of the awkward transition. With a heavy thrust, I feigned left before digging into the mat with my feet and shoving into his chest, directly over his heart.

Izzy jumped up and started dancing around. "Hell yes, that's my girl!"

It was weird to have someone cheering me on for killing a fake vampire, but I couldn't deny that her unusually peppy support made the victory even sweeter—so long as I swallowed the memory of what had distracted me in the first place.

I took a faux bow and winked at her. "Anything, for my adoring fans."

Atlas tilted his head down, swiping the weapon away as if it were nothing more than a feather. "That wasn't great, but it's better than what you've been giving me most of the day. Go get cleaned up and eat. You'll pick this up again tomorrow."

15

DECLAN

"Hey Declan," a soft voice echoed behind me. I was still chewing the last bite of my food as I left the dining hall. There were enough people around that I could pretend I didn't hear anyone and keep walking. Today was a day from fucking hell and all I wanted was to try and get a few decent hours of sleep before I had to go through it all again. Was I technically an instructor right now? Yes. Did that mean I wanted to talk to the students after hours? Abso-fucking-lutely not.

I pushed the heavy door open into the dark night. Hopping down the stairs three at a time, out of habit, I scanned the wooded boundaries surrounding me. My body seemed cloaked in an extra layer of hypervigilance these days, and I couldn't shake the fear that pretty soon we'd see an attack on campus. If vamps were already getting ballsy enough to attack in our town, it was only a matter of time.

I pressed my eyelids together, trying desperately to erase the image of Max, covered in blood when Atlas had carried her home. While I could usually push the images away during the day, in my dreams, her languid battered body was constantly interchanged with Sarah's. It was beyond maddening.

An annoying set of steps behind me clued me in to the fact that my shadow wasn't leaving me. Just my luck. Stopping short, I spun around, the force of a solid body drawing a surprised breath from me. "What the hell?"

"I'm so, sorry. Are you okay?"

Speak of the devil. I looked down into a pair of dark brown eyes set into an oval face with high cheekbones. She was still caked in sweat from the intense bout with Atlas, flyaway hairs curling around her forehead like a crown.

"Max," I acknowledged reluctantly. She was still in my space, so all I could focus on was her presence. She was about a head shorter than me, and the warm vanilla scent of her hair surrounded me in a cloud. I breathed in through my mouth, trying to ignore the fact that it wasn't the worst scent I'd ever smelled before. "What do you want? Can this wait until tomorrow?"

She took a step back, breathing in and out a few times. Her eyes narrowed slightly and she looked everywhere but in my eyes. Instead, her focus landed just north, like she wanted the illusion of eye contact. Why?

"Look, I'm really bad at this sort of thing." She shook her head softly, sweeping a few strands of hair away from her face. "This morning, I was a complete ass. I shouldn't have snapped at you like that. It's just—these past few days have been a lot. And I'm trying to adjust to this," she swept her arm out to the side in a lazy gesture, "whole place, but it's a lot. I'm not the type of person who snaps at other people. I don't usually have a temper at all, really, so—"

"Max"

"Yeah?"

"Breathe." I bit back a grin. Her presence was like an intoxicating cloud of happy that I couldn't seem to get away from.

She chuckled softly, her cheeks reddening a bit with embarrassment. "Right. Sorry. I tend to ramble. It's a bad habit. One that I'm trying desperately to break." For the first time since she chased me down, her eyes met mine. There was something so inviting about the way she looked at me, so open. "I just wanted to say that I was sorry. I was frustrated this morning about Ralph and I shouldn't have taken that frustration out on you. You've been nothing but kind to me since I got here."

Kind? That wasn't a word I would use to describe my actions. Not a word anyone would use in association with me.

I studied her for a moment, watching the way she tried to calm her breathing back down before she got flustered again.

"It's okay. Thank you for apologizing—" I paused, looking up to see that Atlas was standing in the entryway, watching us. His head was cocked at an angle, and I knew that he was listening to every word we said, even though he was a good twenty feet away.

Insufferable prick.

"I'm sorry too," I added, surprising myself. "I don't think any of us really realized how difficult your transition into this life-style would be. It's a lot. I can see that. And you haven't exactly had an easy week, even from a protector standpoint."

The right side of her lips quirked up in a small smile and she scratched the back of her neck. Her eyes roamed around the woods, like she was searching for something to say. Some sort of answer. "Thank you."

With a grin of my own, I nodded before turning around. I took a few paces towards the cabin, not bothering to wait for Atlas to catch up. He was my best friend, but that sometimes made it harder to be around him. Since Sarah's death, we both had a shared grief—a kind that shrouded us when we were together and refused to be ignored. Masks only worked around people who didn't know to look under them.

"Would you—" Max called behind me, stopping me in my tracks. "Er, would you maybe want to hang out?"

I turned around, stunned. Aside from the fact that she was a few years younger than me, I wasn't exactly the 'hanging out' type. Everyone knew that. Everyone who knew me anyway. Sarah was the life of the party, the one person in my life who constantly tried dragging me to parties and social events. With her gone, I didn't even bother seeking out company beyond Atlas and the rest of the team.

"Hang out?" I echoed, the words a bit more harsh than I'd intended.

"Um, yeah. I don't really have a lot of friends here and you seem cool. Izzy—you know Izzy right? Well she's going to come hang with me and Ro. She wants to do a vampire pop culture marathon in honor of, you know, me surviving the attack. I know that probably sounds kind of strange, but I'm into the irony of it all. And laughing can be a good balm. Do you want—would you like to join us?"

A vampire pop culture marathon. I discreetly brushed my hand along my lips, just to make sure my mouth wasn't hanging open. I didn't want to be rude. But a girls' movie night wasn't exactly my thing. I started to shake my head, prepared to politely turn down the offer, when my eyes caught on Atlas. His head shook, the movement so subtle I only caught it out of familiarity. Atlas was the closest thing I had to family. I knew his body language—thoughts, even—better than I did my own.

He wanted me to go. To befriend Max. Get an in with her so that we could keep better track of her, maybe even figure out more about her and her family. Overnight, she'd become a mission. Another thing for him to obsessively pour all of his energy into. And I would help. Of course I would. That's what family was for. Failure was an impossible thing for protectors to recover from.

So, instead of throwing a 'why me' temper tantrum in the middle of the grounds, I settled for shooting him one of my death glares, braided with the silent promise of retribution.

He narrowed his eyes, his face shifting into that dickish smirk of his, before he went back into the building, disappearing from sight. He knew he'd won, he didn't need to stick around to watch the outcome unfold.

"I mean, you don't have to if you don't want to," Max said,

getting flustered by my silence. "Sorry, it was probably silly of me to assume you didn't have better things to do with your night."

Better things? Not unless you counted poring over report after report from every werewolf reconnaissance in the last decade with Atlas.

"Anyway, have a good night," she said, turning back towards the building, her shoulders rounded slightly in defeat.

I exhaled, a weird part of me sorry to see her so dejected. "Max, wait."

She spun around, her eyes sparkling with curiosity.

"Let me go rinse off." Despite my reluctance, I felt a smile unexpectedly start to carve across my face. "But yeah, a pop culture moviethon, or whatever the hell you called it sounds...nice. I'll be up in an hour."

☙❧

"God he's beautiful," Rowan groaned. His legs were bent over the arm of the couch, his head resting in Max's lap while she absentmindedly ran her fingers through his hair. Their relationship was so easy, so warm. They were closer even than Sarah and I were, maybe even closer than Wade and Atlas.

My stomach tightened at the love between them, the absolute trust.

"You can't be serious?" I straightened up, accidentally brushing Max's knee with my own. We both stilled at the contact.

Three episodes of The Vampire Diaries in and I wasn't hating my night of babysitting as much as I thought I would. The show was absolutely ridiculous, but it was weirdly fun listening to everyone's commentary.

"You know, Damon kind of looks like a male version of you," Izzy said, her perfectly-groomed right brow arching as she smirked. "So I would take it as a compliment that we all think he's hot."

Max coughed out a laugh and turned to face me, her brown eyes studying me with a renewed focus. I could feel my face warm from the attention, and I found myself suddenly hating my pale skin. Irish roots made it difficult to disguise embarrassment.

"Yeah, he kind of does. You both have that dark hair, green eyes, loner, rebellious thing going for you." Max broke off when Rowan nudged her knee with his fist. She paled a bit, her eyes wide with concern. "Sorry, I meant that as a compliment. Not loner in like a bad way. You're the cool kind of loner. The badass sort. Not the creepy or weird kind of loner."

I bit back a grin, watching her stumble over her words. It was weirdly endearing—a sentiment that bugged me, like an itch I couldn't quite scratch.

"The guy's killed a handful of people already, how can any of you find him attractive?" Damon was back on screen, blood dripping down his chin. "Plus he's deliberately fucking with his family. I don't understand why human media glamorizes vampirism. Between shows like this and the movies with the biters who sparkle, it's a miracle real vamps don't capitalize on their popularity and just lure teen girls in by the droves."

"I don't know," Max started, her knee bouncing up and down slightly against mine. "The murder is definitely bad, of course. But it's kind of interesting that human media tends to explore the complexities of monsters. They aren't all good or all bad, you know?" She flung her hair up into a messy bun, sending another cloud of her vanilla shampoo into the air. "It's cool that the characters have the same complexities and shades of gray as we do— makes the stories more interesting to follow. It makes them, I don't know—feel?" She bit her bottom lip softly, and I forced myself to focus elsewhere.

"Plus vampire stories have traditionally been used as metaphors for thinking about humanity's fear of the other." Izzy said, shrugging as she flung through the pages of a magazine. I studied her until she lifted her eyes and glanced at us. "What? I'm a big fan of Dracula."

"Real vampires are all bad," I said, my voice low. "They kill humans and protectors indiscriminately. It's how they're built and people should fear them. I would think after your experience last weekend, that would be more clear," I said, watching Max out of the corner of my eye. While I agreed with what I was saying, I found myself digging my heels in more than I usually would. Debating them and discussing humanity's misconceptions about vampirism was weirdly entertaining.

She stilled, and I could feel her muscles tense up against me. "That's the nature of a metaphor though, right? It doesn't have to represent every truth, just any truth. Don't worry though, Declan," she flung her brother's head away and drew her knees to her chest. "I'm under no illusions that vampires are secretly capable of being saved." She shivered slightly, before turning towards me again. "And what's more, I met one in the dungeon when I visited Ralph, so I'm officially doubling down on vamps having a creepy vibe."

"Ooh, I almost forgot about the hot vamp you ran into," Izzy said, flipping a page as she chuckled. "Shame that beauty so often gets wasted. Still, it doesn't hurt to have eye candy, so long as no one gets close enough to try and take a bite." She looked up at me and winked. "Pun intended."

I ran my fingers over the small half-moon marks my nails had dug into the soft flesh of my palm. The casual debate was hitting too close to home now. One breath in, one breath out. "You shouldn't be down there, Max." I didn't want to boss her around, especially not when I'd been almost enjoying the night so far. But she had no idea how dangerous the creatures down there were. "Vampires are dangerous. But the ones down in the lab are next level."

"How so?" she asked, angling her body towards mine. "They're kept in a prison, so it's not like they can get out and attack."

"The Guild only keeps the creatures worth studying alive. Typically that tends to mean the strongest and smartest. And the vampires down there spend all of their time in the belly of their enemies, watching protectors day in and day out. Vampires are evil, but they aren't unintelligent." I took another breath, trying to steady my voice, remove the emotion from it. This wasn't like me, it felt like my emotions were slowly leaking out of me, fit to burst. "On more than one occasion, the creatures down there have manipulated the scientists and caretakers who watch over them."

Max narrowed her eyes, the show providing an odd sound-track to our conversation. "What do you mean? Like manipu-lated researchers into letting them out?"

"Dec—can I call you Dec? Anyway, Dec's right," Izzy said, her lip tilting into a frown as she studied me with her storm-cloud eyes. It wasn't quite pity in their depths, but something like pity's slightly more tolerable older sibling. My stomach clenched. "It's only happened a few times, but it does happen. The humanoids will occasionally manipulate a researcher into letting their guard down and then they strike. Best to stay away from them altogether. Vampires are predators in every sense of the term—their beauty, their draw, it can sometimes disguise their danger."

"Field team it is, then," Ro said, a shadow crossing his features even as he smiled. Field work didn't have the highest survival odds for protectors either. A fact that none of us would have the luxury of forgetting. Perhaps it was strange to warn her about viewing the monsters through the protection of glass, when I was training her to one day hunt them down and put them there.

Max stood up and walked over to the kitchen. "Important point. We can just stick to admiring the fictional vampires on TV while hunting down the creepy ass ones in real life. Deal? Because that sounds good to me. Now," she spun around, a gleaming smile on her face as the discomfort of the conversation melted away. How did she do that? Against my better judgment, my own irritation and tension evaporated too. "Who wants popcorn? I'm starving."

"Fuck yes," Izzy said, tossing her magazine on the floor, the pages cascading in a puddle. "Triple butter. Or ice cream. Actually, fuck the or, let's do both."

They started laughing and clamoring in the kitchen, the sound of their chatter washing over me like a strange warm light. Rowan's eyes met mine with a grin, and we shared one of those looks that screamed 'if-you-can't-beat-em-join-em.' It was just a moment, but it felt like a silent invitation into their world, their group. Maybe girls' night wasn't the worst assignment I'd ever been given.

16

MAX

"Why don't you start at the beginning." Wade twirled his pencil around each of his fingers while he studied me intently. "That way I can get a feel for how much you know and where we should begin." The sentence rang with a slight inflection, like he was asking a question, unsure of the right way to start.

"Do you tutor people often?" I asked, trying desperately to avoid looking at his face for too long. Being in an empty classroom with no one but him was intimidating as hell. I didn't need to be reminded of exactly how beautiful he was or the fact that the last time we were together, he'd tried to drunkenly kiss me. My stomach was filled with enough nerves as it was. Nervous energy just seemed to be constantly oozing out of me like a bad odor these days.

"That obvious?" He grinned, scratching the top of his head. "You're my first student, officially anyway. I've got a knack for books and stuff, so I helped a lot of my friends while I was taking classes."

"You're doing great!" I rushed out, wanting to comfort his own anxiety. It was an empty compliment, we hadn't even started really. But if I couldn't calm my nerves, maybe I could soothe his.

"The beginning is probably a perfect place to start." I closed my eyes desperately trying to forget about how warm his lips had felt against my cheek. "Cy has always been really tight-lipped about this world. So we were never given much more than the bare bones, although I learned a few things from Ro since he lived with his parents for a few years."

"Sometimes I forget that you and Rowan aren't actually related." Wade dipped his brow low and sunk back against his chair. "What happened to his original guardians?"

"Raid," I said, not elaborating. It wasn't something that Ro spoke about often—his life before I entered it. I wasn't even really sure how much he remembered about that life. And I wasn't comfortable spreading what little information he'd shared with me in the first place. His secrets were stored inside of me, guarded in a vault. It had been that way since the day he came out to me, his breath held tight like he was terrified I'd be disappointed. It would be that way until I died.

Wanting to keep the conversation away from things that weren't really my business, I thought back to Wade's question. "I know that protectors evolved from angels, and that they were left on earth to kill off demons and creatures from the hell realm. That vampires and werewolves are the most common creatures identified in our own world, and the ones we will spend most of our time hunting."

And judging by my recent personal experience, it seemed that was pretty accurate.

Wade stared at me for a moment, like he expected me to continue on. "Er, that's all the information he's given you?"

I shrugged, trying to ignore the sting of Cyrus's secrecy. "I mean I know how to kill wolves and vampires, in terms of stabbing in the heart or decapitating, and that humans can't be turned. But no, not much more."

He exhaled, shoving away the stack of books he'd brought with him. "Okay, then we should definitely start at the *beginning,* beginning then." His blue eyes flashed in my direction, a grin dancing in their depths. "But don't worry, I'll get you caught up."

Excited by the prospect of finally learning about the world I'd been sheltered from for so long, I sat up straighter, attentive. For the moment, I'd shove away thoughts about Cy and why he had sheltered us in the first place. If he wanted us to survive in this world, he had to know that knowledge was our best shot, right?

"Protectors evolved from angels, that much is true," Wade started, tracing a timeline onto a fresh sheet of paper. His writing was neat, precise. "But maybe devolved is the better phrasing to use. The kind of magic that we have, it's not infinite. Throughout the years, angels have expended most of their energy protecting humans from demons—so much so that each hundred years or so, our magic seems to grow weaker and our numbers grow smaller."

I thought back to my classes, the bond ceremonies, and the general sausage fest on campus. "Is that connected to why there are so few female protectors left? And why there are bonds?"

Wade moved his head from side-to-side, somewhere between a yes and a no. "Kind of. Generally, it's agreed that the reason we have so few women is connected. And the number of successful protector pregnancies gets lower each generation as well. Contemporary mating bonds in our society are connected more to necessity for those reasons. But bondmates were a thing from the very beginning—they just used to happen organically and for the sake of genuine affection and community. It was how families were built. Teams and bonds were the foundation of our culture. Now, it's how we survive."

I narrowed my eyes, not wanting to seem too cynical. "How do you know for sure? I mean marrying for love is a fairly new concept for humans; it seems suspect that angels were so ahead of that curve centuries ago."

He bit his bottom lip, the white of his teeth standing out against his smooth skin. "That's a good point. To be honest, who knows. History books are written by the victors and social norms. It's entirely possible that we don't concretely know much about where we come from. Our mythology in many ways, is no more confirmed than any human spiritual belief." With a clear of his throat, he focused back on track. "Anyway, for centuries, bonds have been created as a way to keep protectors alive. Kind of like built-in protection. And a different sort of family."

For a moment, he withdrew slightly, like a sadness was creeping over him that he couldn't quite keep at bay. The thought of being magically bound to someone else still freaked me the fuck out, but the way that Eli, and now Wade phrased it, I could almost see the appeal. Family. Community. Those were things I craved something fierce. I wouldn't give up Cy or Ro for anything, but the thought of having more people that mattered to me—that I mattered to. Well, it wasn't the worst thing.

I thought back to Wade's first point, trying to avoid the doom that seemed to come with it. If we were slowly losing our abilities and our strengths...and if our numbers were diminishing, how much longer did humans stand a chance? I still didn't agree with the lab downstairs and how things were being run there in terms of Ralph, but I was starting to understand how so many protectors justified it. The urgency was real, tangible. Fear made people act in ways they weren't always proud of. "This slow decay of the protector line—"

"Depressing way of phrasing it, but not incorrect."

"Does it have to do with the increase in supernatural activity that I keep hearing about?" And experiencing first hand, but I didn't see the need to bring that up again.

"Yep," Wade said, his entire face lighting up like a damn Christmas tree.

I tried not to stare, but when Wade smiled it was like the whole world spun around me. Still... "Kind of a weird thing to be happy about."

He chuckled and shook head. "No, you misunderstand. I'm not happy about that. I'm impressed. You've been paying attention. And you're making important connections even though this is all so new to you."

I tried to disguise how pleased I was at his words. While I didn't always know how to navigate social situations, I loved learning—and being valued for that made me embarrassingly gooey inside. "Thanks, you're a good tutor. I mean, don't get me wrong, I still feel like I'm three laps behind where I need to be, and about a hundred laps behind everyone else...but this kind of context is really helpful for understanding how this world works. I think these sessions will help me feel more at home here."

Part of me didn't want to get too attached to this place, to this whole world. It was all still so new, and chaotic. I was terrified that I would hate living here with so many people, in a world that turned mine completely upside down. But at the same time, I didn't want to get too comfortable. I couldn't quite explain it, but part of me was terrified that I would find a new version of home here, only for it to be ripped away before my eyes.

I thought back to the vamp outside of Vanish. "It's rare, right? Vamps coming so close to the grounds here?" I waited for his nod before continuing. "Do we—" I paused, feeling weird about including myself. "I mean, does anyone know why the supernatural activity has been increasing so much?"

"If they do, they're not sharing the knowledge publicly," Wade said, his voice laced with a frustration that was completely at odds with his excitement from a few moments ago. I wondered, briefly, how much infighting there was amongst all of the protectors. "But they're trying to rush teams through, get as many students graduated as possible to help push things back. This past year especially has been like trying to stop a waterfall with nothing but your hands."

"When do people usually graduate? Join teams?" And, though I didn't say it, how could I make sure that I was with Ro?

"Historically, at twenty or twenty-one. But there's talk that it's shifting. Tensions are high." He hunched slightly, his crystal eyes piercing mine. "And you didn't hear it from me, but I think soon enough they're going to push people through at nineteen. Maybe even earlier."

I was almost nineteen, and Ro already was. The thought of him going on missions, fighting against an unstoppable deluge of supernaturals without me turned my stomach to a block of ice. I came out alive after my last two encounters with the hell realm, but both experiences made it overwhelmingly clear how very fragile protectors were in this fight.

"Each generation, they move the timeline back just a touch. Nineteen used to be more important as an age bracket, it's when protectors fully came into their powers and the extra years learning to harness them were really valuable. Now that those powers are diminished, it's more of a symbolic nod to history than anything. Nineteen brings little more than slightly heightened senses. From birth, we're stronger and faster than humans. That boosts a bit more as we transition into maturity. But our power never rivals the creatures from hell. Not one-on-one."

I thought back to Ro's birthday, the way that Cy spent the evening studying him and watching us as we sparred throughout the day. It made sense why he splurged and got Ro a new set of daggers. That birthday was its own graduation of sorts, a commemoration into adulthood, the way that eighteen was for humans. I looked forward to my own. The more power that I had, the more strength—the better chance I had of protecting the people I cared about.

"Do we," I started, my skin buzzing with anxiety and an unwelcome layer of guilt. "Do we have any say about which team we join when we graduate?" It seemed like an uncommonly big ask—to trust a group of people so completely.

Wade's fingers twitched, inching over slightly across the table so that our pinkies were a mere breath away from each other. There was something so oddly intimate about the gesture that I found myself unable to pull away. Our eyes met and he smiled, small lines crinkling the sides of his mouth.

"The Guild leaders in charge of making determinations take

chemistry into consideration when placing students," he said, his face leaning towards mine ever so slowly.

Our pinkies met and it was like an explosion took off underneath my skin at the point we touched. The draw I felt when around Wade was intoxicating. It was too much, too confusing. It was like there was a string or magnet slowly pulling us together, and each time we got close, the magnet strengthened.

I inhaled sharply, pulling away. To be honest, I was surprised I had the power to do it, to not just surrender to the pull. My heartbeat hammered embarrassingly against my ribcage.

His lips turned down slightly but he didn't say anything, clearing his throat as he turned a page in one of his books instead. The moment was broken, and silence filled the room like a heavy, unwelcome coat. At a sharp knock, my head whipped towards the door, the momentum creating a small crack in my joints.

"Atlas," I said, the sight of him standing there, watching us intently, had my chest clenching uncomfortably. For some reason, I had the undeniable feeling that I'd done something wrong—even though I hadn't done anything at all.

He crossed his arms as he leaned against the doorframe, a tightness in his expression as he stared at his brother.

Wade cleared his throat, pushing back from the table, creating several inches of space between us. The air in the room suddenly seemed filled with a frost.

"Declan mentioned that you two were studying in here," he said, taking a few brisk steps into the room. His eyes stayed on his brother, barely paying me any mind. While I empathized with the stare he leveled at Wade, it was nice, for once, not to be the recipient of it.

"What's up?" There was a coolness to Wade's tone as he tapped his pen against the table.

Clack, clack, clack.

The sound matched my pounding heart, beat for beat.

"We're leaving in the morning," Atlas said, finally glancing in my direction, even if briefly. "Jer and Arnell will be prepped on my expectations for your training, Bentley."

"Not you and the rest of Six?" I asked, trying to stifle the weird feeling overcoming me. Was that disappointment? Was I becoming a masochist? I should be pleased that I'd get a break from Atlas's relentless scrutiny during my sparring sessions.

"Don't get too down, beautiful," Eli piped up as he crowded into the room. He was so silent in his entrance, that I didn't even notice he was trailing behind Atlas until he spoke. "I know no one can compare to us, but you'll be in good hands. We have a mission to prepare for tomorrow."

My head swung around to him, taking in his dark expression that was more serious than usual, underneath the playful tone he liked to lace around everything he said. The more I got to know him, the more it seemed like a defense mechanism, a way to distract people from looking too closely.

"What kind of mission?" I asked, my curiosity piqued.

"Not your concern," Atlas said, his words closed off and cold —any progress I'd made with him over our last session seemed to instantly dissolve. Great, was this how it was always going to be with him?

"Did you push for this?" Wade ground out, his eyes narrowed like a cat at his brother. "Are you certain this is the best time?"

The two brothers were locked in a wordless battle, Wade's crystal depths against Atlas's brown chasms.

I turned back towards Eli, figuring I could get more out of him than I would out of either of them. "Can Ro and I go?"

Eli pushed himself off the wall, squaring off with me. "Absolutely not. You're a student. You stay in bounds at all times unless given express permission otherwise."

"But we could help," I said, "isn't that the whole point of training us? We're good fighters. And I survived one attack solo." Eli arched an amused brow but I ignored him. I mean, yeah, I survived because of Ralph, but still, I held my own for a bit. "If we're part of a team, what happened outside of Vanish won't happen again. I was taken by surprise and didn't have backup."

For some reason, I couldn't bring myself to voice the concern that one of them would be hurt. Partially because the fear surrounded me in such a heavy, unexpected flare up. When did Six sink underneath my skin? I didn't know them very well at all —in fact I avoided Atlas whenever possible. But still, I couldn't shake the feeling that came over me, the absolute certainty that they were going to be confronting an acute danger. One that I could help stave off if I was given the opportunity.

"No," Atlas said. He took a step towards me, his eyes boring into mine. It took everything I had not to step back and wilt under his glare. Something about looking into his eyes made me feel like I was inches away from diving off a cliff. "You are not now, nor will you ever be a member of our team, Bentley. The sooner you understand that, the better things will go for you."

⚜ 17 ⚜

ELI

Three hours into the plane ride and I was in desperate need of a xanax. Flights were my least favorite part of being a protector. Seriously, metal contraptions that weighed several tons had no business flying through the atmosphere. Humans were an odd bunch, but nothing screamed magic as much as when they found a way to defy physics.

But, Atlas's intel swore that our pack of wolves was in the middle of the Midwest, and rather than leave it to one of our satellite groups on the east coast, we were instead on our way to clean up our own mess. He was sitting across from me, pretending to study the books of obsessive notes he'd been taking about recent North American wolf patterns. But his eyes weren't moving, and he hadn't turned the page in half an hour, so I was pretty sure he was as distracted as I was.

A loud pop made us all jump and I looked down at my hand. I'd been clenching my fist so hard that I'd busted the bottle of water I was drinking from.

"You okay, man?" Wade asked, the sound of his voice groggy with disuse. We usually spent long drives and flights going over whatever strategy Atlas had come up with for the specific mission, or at the very least listening to me tell stories about my

most recent girl troubles. No one really cared about my sexca-
pades of course, but distracting me with boobs was the best way
to keep my flight anxiety down.

Today was different and I had a feeling that the thing
rubbing me the wrong way was having a similar effect on the
guys.

Max Bentley.

Generally, I didn't pay much attention to the students at the
academy, at least not beyond training and assisting with various
fighting demos. There was the occasional girl I'd have my eye on,
but those infatuations never lasted more than a few days.

But something about Max just dug into my attention span
unlike anyone or anything else before. It was like as soon as she
arrived at The Guild, everything had been skewed off center.
There was a weird draw to her and I was half convinced she was
secretly a succubus or something. If she weren't so socially
awkward, I'd be fully convinced.

And the vampire attack at Vanish wouldn't stop skating
through my mind. After a single day on campus she'd nearly died.
You pretty much had to *try* to have luck that rotten.

Not to mention my father wouldn't spill any information
about her or where they'd been living for the last two decades.
He wasn't one for keeping secrets from me, which just made me
want to know all the more. It was fucking infuriating. Instead,
Max was dangled in front of me like a sexy carrot, perpetually
out of reach.

"You hear anything from your aunt or the other researchers
about the vamp that attacked Max, Dec?" Wade asked, glancing
at her briefly while he stared out the window like a wide-eyed
puppy. He loved flying. One of the many things I didn't understand about the kid.

Declan's eyes were closed and she was even more quiet
than usual. She wasn't particularly close to her aunt, especially
since Sarah died, but she tried to check in every couple of
weeks. Sarah loved her mom and it would've broken her heart

to see Dec permanently pull away from the only family she had left.

Her aunt had been our strongest ally in the research quarters, so it sucked when she transferred to the European Headquarters after the funeral. Our base held too many memories of her daughter for her to stick around without losing her sanity. Truthfully, I had no idea how Dec could stand it. Or any of them really. I was the least close with the girl, and even I had trouble living down the hall from her old room.

She shook her head. "No man, she called several of the contacts here that she trusts but they said they still haven't found anything unusual about the vamp or his venom. They've done a full autopsy and can't understand how she healed so quickly. But they lifted her skin cells from his teeth, so she was definitely bitten."

My stomach clenched at the last part, my blood boiling like lava through my veins. Would she have been attacked if I wasn't fucking around, making her uncomfortable? My father asked me to watch out for her, to be a sort of guide into our life here. And my first night on the job she became a vamp snack.

"And the hound?" I asked, no longer even pretending to be engrossed by the game on my phone.

I met Atlas's eyes and he frowned. Atlas knew that the researchers were going to town with tests on the creature. Like me and Cyrus, he was fighting to get the beast released. Or at least put on a longer leash. If Max kept sneaking down there, we'd have to alter the footage on the cams every night. It was dangerous. For all of us. And while Atlas, Wade and I were convinced that the beast wouldn't hurt Max, my father and Declan weren't so trusting.

Dec shook her head, the ripples of her hair catching a few rays of sun. "Nothing of interest, yet. They're still running tests, but looks like for the moment, they've agreed not to put it down." I shot her a look, my anxiety dislodged by anger. "Don't look at me like I kicked your puppy, Eli. It wasn't my decision either way. Aunt Jay said no protector has ever come across one and lived to tell the tale. Max's beast is the first that's ever been captured. Ever. I don't blame them for wanting to be sure before letting that thing loose. The mythology of the creatures is gruesome and haunting. No one wants to take any chances." She let out a long sigh, her voice softening slightly. "And Max is new to this world. She's incredibly naive. Turning her into a hellhound guinea pig right now is just asking for trouble."

"About Max—" Wade said, making eye contact with Atlas. When Atlas shook his head slightly, Wade ignored him and looked between me and Declan instead. "Have you guys noticed anything different? Felt a pull or anything?"

"Jesus, Wade," Atlas grumbled, running a hand roughly over his face. "I told you to shut up about this ridiculous theory." He unbuckled his seat belt and stood up, before sitting back down, every muscle in his body tensed. "You're not bonding with her."

Legitimate bonding? It *was* a ridiculous theory. Except why did my stomach drop when he voiced it? I'd been internally joking with myself that Max had a draw, but knowing officially that I wasn't the only one to feel it? I didn't know whether to be intrigued, jealous, or deny, deny, deny.

Declan arched one black brow, studying Wade with crystalline focus. "What do you mean, draw?"

"I mean," Wade continued, his voice trembling slightly, "like the early stages of a bond. A real one."

Atlas groaned, dropping his face into his palms.

I held my breath, feeling disturbingly like my heart had sunk to my stomach. "You've been bonded before, mate," I said, keeping my tone light and disinterested. "This how it felt?"

Wade frowned, and shook his head. "Not quite, this feels sort of similar, but completely different at the same time."

Declan squeezed Wade's shoulder. She was always the most affectionate towards him, probably because along with Atlas, she helped raise him. Wade and Atlas had had a hard time after Sarah died. They weren't romantically or sexually involved with her or anything, and their bonded ties were new, fresh, but still—that sort of loss took a toll. From my understanding, losing a bondmate was like losing a part of you. You never got over that sort of pain, like a phantom limb.

And in protector culture, bonds had a way of making your life purpose the protection of your bondmate group. Sarah's death struck them hard and in different ways. Wade just seemed broken, burying his time in his studies, more standoffish and jaded than he used to be; Declan had become more cynical and detached than ever; and Atlas, well, Atlas was obsessed with tracking. He'd even gone out on his own, without us, several times.

I studied him, trying not to look too long at the silver scar on his arm. Atlas had been one of my best friends since we were teenagers, but not even I could get him to open up about Sarah. He'd become even more of a machine after that, obsessed with keeping the team on track and safe, determined to at least protect Wade—if not from their father, from everyone else.

Part of me was almost jealous of their shared bond, their shared grief. Which was extremely fucked up and I lost my appetite every time the feeling flitted through my thoughts, unwelcome as all get out.

I opened my mouth, then shut it again. "Look, I'm not *not* saying I feel a certain pull."

Declan's head snapped over to me, a tense smirk across her face. "Eli, you feel a certain pull to literally every female you encounter."

"Except to you, babycakes," I winked.

"Small mercies." The tension in her grin melted away into genuine fondness. Dec and I had a weird relationship. And she was living proof that I was capable of a platonic relationship with a woman. A shock to us all, because Dec was fine as fuck. It probably had more to do with the fact that we were both competing for female affections.

Atlas laughed, but the smile didn't reach his eyes. Did he feel drawn to Max too? I narrowed my eyes at him, studying his even-more-tense-than-usual posture. He'd been an absolute prick since Max had arrived, and the way he'd been pushing her away? Maybe. It wasn't impossible. But he was impossible to read these days.

"I know, I know, but in all seriousness." I cleared my throat awkwardly. "I mean, I'm definitely pulled to her in terms of attraction. The girl's hot. But there's something else too, something I'm not used to."

Declan's expression darkened slightly, and I studied Atlas as he studied her. The two of them always had a way of talking in silence. It was a system of subtle cues and hidden depths that I wasn't privy to. But judging by the blood draining from his face, he didn't like the outcome of her thoughts.

Curious.

With a quick nod, as if giving himself a pep talk, Atlas straightened up, officially abandoning his notebooks. "Look, I don't know what exactly it is about her, but I don't trust it. Cyrus shows up after almost two decades, bringing with him two random orphans? Not buying it, especially since Eli's dad has been trying to get him back here for years. Between that and the increased activities, I just don't think it's wise to act on anything."

"But—" Wade opened his mouth, clearly ready to protest.

"I'm not saying she's evil or anything, Wade. Just that things are complicated right now. Bonds are active creations, so even if you're right—which I highly doubt in this case—we have the power to stop their manifestation," Atlas said, cracking his neck side to side, like he was uncomfortable in his own skin. I didn't blame him, the plane was starting to feel smaller than usual.

"I'm going to be real honest, dear old Seamus has hinted more than once that he wants me to consider bonding to her an option down the line," I said, allowing myself to admit the possibility out loud for the first time. It wasn't an idea that I was particularly comfortable with. I wanted the girl out of my thoughts, not forced more deeply into my very existence. Bonding with someone like Dec would be so much easier—we'd go in knowing exactly where we stood. The boundaries would be clear as day.

"Down the line could be years from now, mate" Dec said as she leaned forward, her elbows pushing down on her knees. "I agree with Atlas on this. She's new. Rowan's new. We need to keep them at more than an arm's length."

"Big surprise there." I muttered, not bothering to hide the frustration from my laugh.

Her fingers gripped the arms of my chair. "What the hell is that supposed to mean?"

I shrugged, cocking an eyebrow and turning towards her. "Nothing, just that first of all, you always agree with Atlas, and second of all, it's not exactly difficult to convince you to push people away. Sort of your MO, *mate*."

She unbuckled her seatbelt, tension visibly clawing through her body. She and Atlas were so similar sometimes, so uncomfortably blocked up. They both could do with an emotional laxative.

"Enough," Atlas said. "This is what I mean. The stakes are too high for us to lose focus right now."

Wade opened his mouth to argue again, but Atlas turned to him. "Besides, it's not safe for Max to get too close with our group right now."

Understanding filled the suddenly crowded cabin, and Wade and I backed off a bit, though I could tell that he was still silently stewing in his seat.

I exhaled, bouncing my knee a few times. "Sorry, Dec, heat of the moment. Didn't mean to be a dick, think my sleep schedule has just been off. Or I need to get laid, let off some steam or something."

She nodded, turning back towards Atlas. "Fine, from here on out, Max is one of our recon projects, but nothing more. We get an in, try to learn something, keep an eye on her, but nothing deeper than that. She remains at arm's length."

That was that then, it was agreed upon. My chest tightened. This was what I had wanted all along, a reason to force her out of my thoughts, so why did I suddenly feel so uncomfortable with the idea of not pursuing her?

18

WADE

The four of us had been silently waiting on top of an old industrial building for what felt like hours. Boredom didn't even begin to describe things.

I dug my fingers into the cold metal lining the roof, trying to stave off the evening's chill. The neighborhood was largely abandoned, with walls painted in graffiti tags and crumbling cinder blocks. So abandoned, that the only movement we'd seen took the form of an obnoxiously drunk dude pissing on the side of the building across the street. He sang loudly while trying to draw some sort of smiley face with his urine. The zoom lenses on our cameras meant that we could see every detail while we studied the area around us, and the microphones we'd rigged around the neighborhood meant that we could hear every splatter. The smell was pungent as fuck, even from here. Times like these, I hated having heightened senses.

Sure, humans wanted supernatural powers, but they didn't consider the bad along with the good.

After the plane ride over, we'd all agreed to stop talking about Max. Judging by the tension in the group though, I was convinced that no one had stopped thinking about her. Myself included.

Seeing her in that hospital room after the attack, so vulnerable, it was like seeing Sarah all over again. Which was weird, because they looked nothing alike. And I'd be lying if I didn't admit to being interested in Max in a way that I was never really interested in Sarah. At least not to that level.

I'd agreed to stay away from Max as much as possible, but I didn't know how realistic that was if I was being honest with myself. It was weird, having this intense desire to protect someone. Especially since Max could damn well protect herself. Hell, she'd survived a vamp attack and made best friends with a mythical beast all on day one. I was placing bets that she'd be as powerful as Alleva one day, maybe even more so. And unlike Atlas, I wanted to bond to someone again, wanted to feel that sense of purpose. To be needed. Hell, maybe even to be wanted.

As the newest member of the team, I was still in the famed disappointment stage. During my training, I half expected to be fighting down vamps left and right with every mission. I wasn't really prepared for how fucking boring these recon sessions could be. So much waiting. My muscles were tense from trying to move as little as possible, while shoving my orbital bones against various lenses, trying to catch a glimpse of...something.

But I was bored, and antsy. We were gone for a handful of hours and I was already itching to get back. Something just didn't *feel* right, not about this mission, and not about leaving Max unprotected at The Guild. I couldn't put my finger on it. She'd survived the vamp attack, I'd gotten lucky with that. I didn't want to drop the ball again. Seamus put us in charge of her safety for a reason, and it felt like we were abandoning our primary assignment for something ephemeral. Hell, at this point, who even knew if we'd end up seeing any action at all. Our sources had been wrong before. Many times.

"You sure this is the spot," I asked, impatience making my skin crawl. "Maybe it's a few streets over?"

Atlas shook his head, not even bothering to look at me. I

hated being written off like that, and he was better than most at making me feel like a useless addition to the team.

"No, it's here," he said, his words the ghost of a whisper. "I'm sure of it."

Maybe he could hear something we couldn't. His senses far outstripped ours, so all I could do was bite my tongue and get back to crouching against the gravel and broken slats of the roof floor.

Eli met my eyes, concern coloring his features as he locked eyes on Atlas's scar. He swallowed hard before he nodded once. "Then we wait."

We both knew the truth, that Atlas had been obsessing over this particular wolf pack since Sarah's death. He'd lost her and a part of himself to them and while he liked to pretend he didn't give a shit about Sarah, I didn't think he'd let himself process his pain until he took this pack out. Grief was a fickle bitch; it took you down in unimaginable ways, no story of pain the same.

"Holy shit," Declan muttered, pulling the binoculars flush against her eyes. "Are those vamps?"

She nodded towards a building a block or two away, her lenses pointed at a window on the second floor.

"What?" Atlas asked before grabbing her binoculars away with force.

No fucking way. Vamps and werewolves working together? Since when? As far as protector intel went, they seemed to be apathetic towards each other at best, sworn enemies at worst. They killed each other with more success than we could boast. This, this was new. And big.

I saw the decision flash across Dec's face about a nanosecond before she started to run towards the fire escape.

"Fuck," I muttered, going after her. Where Atlas had a weakness with wolves, Dec was the same with vamps. Quite the group we were, with enough personal vendettas to go around and get us all killed. "Declan!" I whisper-shouted, trying to catch her attention without broadcasting our position. This was not how the plan was supposed to go. We needed to call into The Guild, figure out next steps. We were barely prepared to handle a whole pack of wolves, let alone vamps. And we were on strict recon for this mission. If we spotted the pack, we weren't supposed to attack until backup showed up. "Atlas, let's go," I yelled back behind my shoulder.

"Fuck," Eli echoed, his feet pounding behind mine.

We were temporarily banned from vampire missions, explicitly because of Declan's poor impulse control. Talk about unfinished business. This mission was going south. Fast.

I caught up to Declan outside of the warehouse she'd seen the vamps in. We looked through the first floor windows, able to see what appeared to be six creatures. It was almost impossible to distinguish between vampires and werewolves, unless fangs were descended or a partial shift was occurring. Hell, if Atlas hadn't gone so silent when he stole the binoculars from her, I would've bet money on her seeing things. People saw their demons in everyday moments all the time. But Atlas was better at identifying the different species than we were.

"That one, there," Declan whispered to me, her finger discreetly pointing to a tall guy with red hair, brown eyes, and a poorly groomed beard. "He's vamp, I'm positive. I saw tooth." She exhaled softly, no doubt trying to relax the adrenaline coursing through her body. "Flaccid now though."

"You sure?" I asked, squinting into the room, trying to catch a glimpse. We liked to jokingly call humanoids in pre-shift position flaccid. When they were, werewolves, vamps, succubi, and incubi all pretty much looked the same. They just looked, well, human.

"She's right," Atlas said, annoyance lacing his tone. "I caught a glimpse, must've been feeding. We should call this in."

He was spewing the party line, but I could see the tension in his neck. He was aching for a fight. We all were. I hadn't been on a proper mission in months, our father had made sure of it. And I was so fucking sick of being coddled.

"Or," Declan started, nervously glancing between the three of us. "We can just go in there and knock them out. Try to bring back one of each to Headquarters, get them to figure out what's going on?"

"Might not get another chance," I added, cocking an eyebrow. "We've never seen factions working together before."

"You guys can't be serious," Eli said, looking from me and Declan back to Atlas. "Right, Atlas?" Atlas just looked at him, his lips twitching down in a frown. Eli shook his head, ran his fingers through his hair, and groaned. "Jesus. Fucking. Hell," he muttered to himself. "Fine. Fine, you fucking lunatics. What's the plan then? My dad's going to have my head either way, might as well make it worth it."

The building itself looked practically abandoned, with chunks of concrete missing from the siding every few inches. It also looked like someone had started painting it white years ago, but never got around to finishing; half of the building was an ugly sweat-stain yellow, and half a washed out gray. I scanned around the block, noticing that all of the buildings looked equally shitty. Most of them had holes smashed through the windows and were surrounded by stray bits of grass and debris.

Atlas unstrapped his bag, grabbing a few dart guns to knock them out. The big plan was to separate them and pick them off one-by-one, hopefully from a distance. Atlas and Declan were the most experienced and most capable, so they were going to isolate and tag-team the six humanoid supernaturals in the room we could see, while Eli and I made our way around the building, trying to get a feel for how many others were inside, just to make sure we weren't ambushed.

So basically, Eli and I were on the equivalent of the B team and Atlas and Declan wanted out of babysitting duty. I tried not to bristle at them too much.

Sometimes it fucking sucked being the little brother of one of The Guild's best fighters. Especially now. Atlas was annoyingly protective, and seemed damn convinced that I needed protecting. Even more than usual since Sarah got taken down.

Eli offered a commiserating smile. "Buck up, Wade. Not much fun for us, but this was the right call." He nodded to the right. "I'm going to take this side of the building, you go around the other, yeah?"

Without waiting for a response, Eli started moving, his wavy brown hair disappearing behind the corner.

"Great, yeah, I'll go this way. Super fun," I mumbled to myself. I gripped one of the handles from my set of knives and turned the corner slowly.

The first few windows on my side were pitch-black inside. I could make out the outlines of some furniture, but between the lack of light and the grime covering the inner layer of the glass, I couldn't discern much. In fact, I was starting to think that the only action we were going to see was back with Atlas and Dec, when I noticed a soft yellow glow piercing from the final window. The light wasn't on in the windowed room, but when I pressed closer to the glass, I could see a bright light pooling from behind the room's door, leaking around the frame. Every minute or so, I'd see a shadow move past, like someone was walking by the door. I looked around, considering waiting for Atlas and Declan, or at the very least for Eli. But I was fairly convinced there was only one creature in there. I had my own dart gun, so it shouldn't be difficult to handle it without getting within range of an attack.

Decided, I used the blade of my knife for leverage and lifted the window. Surprisingly, it wasn't locked, just jammed. As quietly as I could, I pulled myself across the splintered frame, sprinkling paint chips and shards of rotted wood with my landing. The room smelled musty, and cobwebs lined each of the corners. Whatever this place was, it was pretty clear that it functioned as a temporary gathering. The vamps and werewolves hadn't done much to spruce it up.

I pressed my ear up to the door, hoping to catch a sound or

conversation. Nothing. I dug my fingernails into my palms when I realized that I'd left my comms device and flashbangs on the roof. Lesson learned. Next time I wouldn't be such a reckless eager fucking beaver.

After another minute, I was convinced the pacer from before had moved on and slowly turned the door knob, pushing it open a fraction. Still nothing. Maybe the guy had gone to help his buddies. Atlas and Dec had to have them just about handled by now. Those two were always such a force when they were working together. Part of me was convinced that if she'd been there the night Sarah was killed, instead of me, that things would have gone very differently.

Satisfied that I was alone, I gripped the dart gun, my finger on the trigger, and opened the rest of the door. I took a step back, trying to figure out what the hell I'd walked in on. It was like stepping through a portal into another world. The room was stunning. A large chandelier hung from the middle of the ceiling, and ornate tapestries decorated the walls. In the center of the room stood a long table, with various papers scattered around amongst what looked to be a fully-catered dinner. I had to stifle a laugh, momentary shocked by the difference between this room and the one I'd just left. Who knew hellbeasts had such snazzy taste after all?

I moved slowly towards the table, resisting the temptation to steal a piece of chicken and glanced at the paperwork. There appeared to be maps of various Guild bases across the world, several of which had a large 'X' drawn across them.

What the hell? I picked up another sheet, finding a long list of names. I didn't recognize many of them, except for two: Connolly and Bentley.

Connolly was Declan's family name.

"The hell are you doing in here, kid?"

I turned around, reaching for a knife with my other hand. A tall man with long blonde hair and a thick beard was in the doorway. Dude looked like he'd walked off of a Viking ship.

Not waiting another moment, I shot a dart, a giant grin stealing across my face as it dug into his chest. Bingo.

As soon as he went down, the dart gun was knocked from my hand. I watched as it went flying into the opposite wall and spun around. Another guy, almost identical in looks to the first was staring daggers at me. I sprang into action, running towards the guy before he doubled back to me. I was always more on the offense side of things, anyway. Fuck the dart gun.

With a quick growl, he lifted a hand—or well, it was a hand until it became a claw. By the time I made it to him, slicing into his chest, he was nearly fully shifted. I missed the heart, unable to determine where it would be while his muscles and bones shifted in painful waves and crunches. Fuck. *Fuck.*

That was the best chance I was going to get and I blew it.

The wolf had to be a solid two-fifty of straight muscle. Bright yellow eyes looked into mine, and I was taken back to my last upfront encounter with a wolf. Was this one of the assholes who killed Sarah? Momentarily filled with rage, I lashed out, slicing into the beast's shoulders and neck. One blade got stuck between two ribs, goring the wolf good, but not doing near enough damage as I needed in order to slow it down. While I tried to dislodge it, the wolf growled and lunged. Sharp teeth clamped on the spot my neck had just been, but I'd dodged just in time.

Not enough though.

I looked down, seeing long claw marks raking down my left arm. I needed to act two seconds ago if I wanted a chance of surviving this. The wolf prepared to snap again but I kicked out at its front leg, smirking when I heard the satisfied snap of bone. With a whine, the animal toppled to the side and, not willing to waste any time, I plunged my knife into his chest cavity. With a shudder rolling through his body, the beast grew still. We wouldn't be bringing this one back with us. But at least I wasn't dead. That would have to be enough.

Staring down at the dead wolf, I thought back to that night

—back to Atlas. It felt different now, wrong almost, killing one of these things. The creature was large, and now that it was no longer trying to attack, it seemed almost peaceful. Why did death have a way of doing that? Of erasing the bad?

This wolf seemed surprised to see me, which meant that Atlas and Declan most likely took down the six in the lobby with no problem. It didn't seem like anyone else in the building was alerted. I could hear nothing but the steady breath pulling from my lungs, in and out. Did we get them all?

Almost as soon as I'd thought the thought—which was my own fault, really—the door swung open.

"Hey Ray, boss—" the girl stopped talking and looked down at the dead wolf I was straddling with absolute horror stretching across her face. "Ray?"

Tears pooled in her eyes as she looked at the wolf, Ray I guess, beneath me. I had a feeling I'd either just killed her boyfriend or else a family member.

Steely resolve transformed her features, her cool blue eyes landing on mine. With a loud battle cry that would've been funny if it weren't filled with so much anguish, she turned towards me. She was maybe fifteen feet away as her muscles began convulsing.

Another one then. Eli was going to be jealous that he was missing out on all the action.

The girl shifted more quickly than I'd ever seen a werewolf shift before. One second she was there, all sad and angry, and then she shimmered like the air on a hot day. Next second, she was a wolf about half the size of her friend, coat as dark black as her hair had been.

And she was already coming towards me at an impressively fast pace. What she didn't have in size, she more than made up for with speed.

I ripped my knife out of the dead wolf's heart, not able to reach a second blade in time from this angle, and turned to face her. Her first move came in hot and I ducked under her without a second to spare. In fact, she'd swiped a nice little scratch into the top of my scalp. She was faster and angrier than her friend had been, so this was unexpectedly going to be more difficult.

I kicked out, aiming for ribs, but she swatted my leg away with a powerful paw. The push caused me to lose my balance, but I still managed to swipe my blade across her neck, drawing a thick line of blood. Not enough to kill her, or even stun her, but it was something.

Only now she seemed even more angry.

Wolves were a lot faster than protectors, and far more powerful. Hopefully Atlas and Declan were done, and on their way to track down me and Eli. If they weren't I was royally screwed.

She rammed me into the long table, scattering the papers and upsetting several platters. A loud clank sounded by my feet, and my hands slid into something with the consistency of mashed potatoes.

Shaking my knife to try and dispel the white chunks, I hit the wolf across the face, wincing slightly. I knew that she was a werewolf and that she was on the bad guy side ride now, but it still felt wrong decking a girl in the face. The momentum of the move had me sliding, my left foot slipping on whatever goop had been knocked over. My nose was filled with the weird combination of iron and starch. It was only a brief second of distraction, but that was all the wolf needed.

Suddenly, I was flipped over the table, my right shoulder slamming at an odd angle against the bulky wood. I stood as quickly as I could, gripping my knife and ready to square off again. Except, my hand wouldn't grip. I looked down, and my stomach sank. My hand was twisted at an off angle and I was pretty sure my shoulder was popped out of the socket. Thank god the adrenaline was high, so I didn't feel too much. My knife clattered to the ground, but I was able to pick it up with my functioning hand.

Only it was slightly too late. Claw marks dug into my side and my neck, like the wolf was trying to give me an overly aggressive and extremely awkward bro hug. I smelled blood, so much blood.

She knocked me off my feet again, using her strength to pin me as she tore into my side. This was it, this was how I was going down. I suddenly wanted to laugh, thinking how senseless I'd been, charging in here solo, with nobody to cover my back. Atlas would blame himself. I didn't know if he could get over my death, if Father would let him. Guilt flooded my belly.

"What's going on in here, Annabelle?" a deep, clear voice echoed around the room.

With a growl turned whimper, she looked towards the door. Neither of us could see the figure from the floor.

Unwilling to waste the opportunity, I bucked my hips to gain some distance and slid my knife into her abdomen. It took less than a second, but I shoved the hilt up, drawing a line through her stomach, eventually embedding the blade into her heart. Her blood, mixed with fleshy ligaments, spilled onto me as her dead weight dropped down.

Gross.

A soft clicking sound echoed across the room, the ominous figure looming closer.

"Everything okay, boss?" a gruff voice echoed. At least three more pairs of feet followed the boss in.

With a deep breath, I closed my eyes, preparing myself to go down fighting. I wouldn't die hiding underneath a wolf carcass. My thoughts flashed briefly to Max and I held onto the image, giving myself permission to linger briefly on her inquisitive eyes and full lips.

I gave myself a second, just one, and then I heaved the body off of me, and jumped to my feet. The bloodied knife made an awful squelching sound as it left Anabelle's chest cavity and I held it to my side, deep red blood covering me from head to toe. I wasn't sure how much of it was mine and how much of it was hers. Right now, I just had to hope that I wasn't too fucked up to get out of here alive.

Just as I'd guessed, four new, enraged faces were positioned by the doors, blocking me in.

No chance of me escaping then. Fuck.

Two of them had eyes locked on the dead wolves, the third pulled back his lips in a deep growl, revealing white pointed canines. Another vamp, then. Great.

My eyes locked onto the final figure, though, and a deep shiver involuntarily crawled up my back. The man was dressed head-to-toe in black, his hair and eyes so deep they almost looked blue. Power radiated off of him and my skin crawled as he studied me, almost as if he could see through me. Where the three others looked ready to murder, this creature appeared almost bored, nothing but an arched brow revealing anything more than apathy towards the situation.

"It appears you clowns have been breached," he said, voice low and cold. The sound alone sent shivers down my spine, filling me with more fear than I could ever remember feeling. He looked up at me, his lips twisting in the shadow of a sardonic grin. "I doubt he's alone, so kill him quickly, I'm sure we'll have more soon. Protectors are like ants, they travel in swarms."

The creatures were hovering in silence until the last syllable echoed through the room. And then, as if in a symphony, they moved as one, two going left and one right.

My only chance was to try and run, but they had me caged in, like a bug in a spider web. I was fucked.

I gripped my knife hard, and ran towards the one, figuring he was my best chance at clearing a path. I'd try and take at least one of them out, maybe two before I went down—give the rest of the guys time to get out and come back with reinforcements so that they could burn this place to the fucking ground. Sometimes it was the only way to get rid of an infestation.

I reached the solo vamp first, using my momentum to slide into his legs, elbowing him in his junk. Generally, it was sportsmanlike to avoid a guy's dick, but this was an emergency and I needed every strategy I could grab. The combination of my weight and his pain knocked him to the ground, and I pulled him on top of me as the two wolves jumped towards us. They ripped into his skin, almost happy to dig through him to get to me. Apparently wolves and vamps weren't working together with quite as much comradery as we feared then. Taking advantage of their confusion, I snapped the vamp's neck, relying on his associates to provide some leverage and slow his response time down. A broken spine wouldn't kill the vamp, but it would stun him for a while and give me time to take on one of the wolves.

Using my legs, I pushed the vamp off of me, unbalancing one of the wolves. Weirdly, they were only partially shifted, but with a growl they simultaneously finished the transformation, like mirror images. With my good arm, I threw my potato-caked knife, smirking when I saw the heavy metal sink into the white wolf's eye, all the way up to the hilt. A loud, venomous roar billowed from the creature, and I watched for a moment as it tried to rip the knife loose.

Taking advantage of the distraction, I ran behind the other wolf. This one was a boring beige. I sunk my fingers into his flank as I tackled him to the ground. His claws ripped into me from at least two places, but I was too high on the fight to feel anything. The white wolf was circling us now, waiting for its chance to join back in and I reached into my boot, pulling out another blade. As his white friend lunged, I sank the silver into the beige wolf's heart.

The wolf was dead, but I didn't have the energy to move off of him, or maybe I'd just lost too much blood and was halfway to dead. My eyes locked onto the fourth man, and saw him watching the scene with casual interest. He clearly didn't mourn the deaths in this room or, if he did, he was excellent at disguising it. Black eyes bored into mine and I watched as the man's nose flared briefly.

Just as the white wolf landed on my back and sank a claw into my already ruined side, the man muttered a soft but firm "stop."

As if programmed, the werewolf removed its paw, one nail at a time, and I felt the shift of weight as it moved away from me.

What the hell? Were they going to kidnap me and keep me in a research dungeon like we did to them? Fear flared through my body, renewed tenfold at the thought. That would be worse than death.

Black boots edged closer, and I watched with morbid fascination as the man stepped into the pool of blood, likely a mingling of three different species. Even so, it all just looked—red.

The man crouched, tilting his head and studying me like I was an interesting exhibit in a modern art museum—the kind you had to pretend to understand. I studied him back, cataloguing his deep olive skin, tailored suit, and stern posture.

He'd avoided the fight today, but I could tell from the intelligence in his eyes as he studied the scene, and in the way that he held himself, that he was a formidable opponent. What *was* he? I wasn't getting wolf or vamp vibes, just raw, unbridled power.

All at once, recognition crossed his dark features and a creepy smile spread across his face.

"How interesting," he whispered, "I see it now."

He reached a hand forward, ready to finish the job. My thoughts drifted to Atlas and the rest of the team. They'd be okay. They'd have had time to get away.

Then I thought of Max, and regret filled my belly, but so did relief—she wasn't here. She was safe, back home. My team would take care of her.

The man's fingers touched the skin of my forehead, heat spreading into my temple, and my body tensed.

His nostrils flared again, jaw muscles tensing before he tilted his body towards the white wolf. "Get our stuff, we're going. Now."

I felt the pressure of strong fingers leave my skull and then, nothing.

FORGING THE GUILD

Grab Book Two in The Protector Guild series:

Creatures from hell are breaching the human world like never before and it's up to The Protector Guild to figure out why.

With Headmistress Alleva back on campus, Max's life at headquarters is thrown upside down. After sightings of werewolves close to Guild boundaries, recruits are thrust into apprenticeships with prominent teams to help move along graduation rates and get them into the field as soon as possible. While this sounds good at first, Max learns that being a protector isn't what she always thought it would be. Increased attacks, mixed with a nefarious research lab that is anything but trustworthy, leaves tensions high and Max desperate for answers.

And if that didn't make things difficult enough, she has to come to terms with her turbulent relationship with the members of Team Six. If the monsters don't destroy her, Atlas, Wade, Declan, and Eli just might finish the job first.

As Max navigates her new role within the Academy, she must

decide who is worthy of her trust. Unfortunately, she learns she can't trust the people she once thought she could...

ACKNOWLEDGMENTS

This book wouldn't be possible without the support from my family and friends. You know who you are and I couldn't be more lucky to have you in my life.

Special thank you to my beta readers, my editor, Kath, and my cover designer, Michelle, from Damoro Design.

And to my very own 'Ralph,' thanks for keeping me company while I wrote for hours on end.

Printed in Great Britain
by Amazon

41628452R00118